# WHERE'S YA MAN?

An Urban Dramedy About
What Life Should Be,
What It Could Be,
And How The Hood Be!

## By Jus One

Printed in the United States of America
First Printing, 2016
This book contains works of fiction.
ISBN 978-0-9983893-0-1
HDB Publishing LLC
Philadelphia, PA 19144
www.HdbPublishing.com
First Edition

For Alym,

"In an attempt to inspire you, you've become my greatest inspiration!"

Daddo

# Chapter One

For several hours the sun had disappeared and was no longer illuminating the sky on America's eastern coast. In the North Philadelphia Badlands section this wouldn't matter much as life would resume outside regardless of light emanating from the sun or reflecting off of the moon. In fact, the sunlight was the only way to tell the day from night in this area as children would play in the street despite the nightfall. To an outsider looking in it might appear that the children had night vision goggles on, but for a North Philadelphia native it was business as usual, deeply interwoven into the fabric of the communities lives. It seemed that in this section of the city the day would be extended by a second sun. This was not the bright yellow ball in the sky that lit up the earth, but rather the Chinese restaurant's bright yellow sign that lit up the corners, allowing life to resume for another six hours in the heart of North Philadelphia. Without warning by way of sunset, the second sun was un-plugged sending the city's residents into their homes for the evening and emanating a sense of calm through out the neighborhood. In the shadows of a now darkened Lehigh Avenue, Eric Garcia affection-ately known as Lil E, born of a Puerto Rican father and an African American mother sits on the front steps of a three story row owned by his grandmother. Despite the many dilapidated houses in this neighbor-hood Lil E could be considered one of the neatest people world over, the type that appears to have been born with a haircut and a new pair of sneakers on. With his cellphone pressed to his face and his eyes on his sneakers he speaks in a moderately quiet tone into his phone

"Aight my nigga, first thing in the AM, yup that'll work...one."

Lil E hangs up his phone and takes the last two pulls from the blunt roach he was smoking. The sound of someone kicking a can a block or two away can be heard on his now desolate street. He takes a hard look at the vacant corner of his block as he stands up and flings the blunt roach into the street before walk-ing up the steps into the large North Philly row home.

Friday morning - Rise & Grind

Several blocks or exactly one train stop away on Allegheny ave, Trina lies stretched out on a queen size mattress on top of an all white sheet set. She is on the brink of being awakened, halfway due to the heat from the sun reflecting through her second floor apartment window directly into her face, and partly due to the time turning from 6:59 to 7:00 triggering the alarm on her smartphone docked in a speaker dock. Monday thru Friday a minute before 7:00 am, she could feel her alarm getting ready to go off. The alarm had become merely insurance for her internal schedule. As her alarm blared she slowly awakens and lifts her phone from inside of the dock on her nightstand. She rolls over and quickly collects herself with a deep breathe and gets out of bed. The slender and extremely attractive twenty-three year old bank teller heads off to the shower to prepare for work. After performing her daily twenty minute shower ritual, Trina exits her steam filled bathroom to get dressed. The bedroom has a theme of dark wood floors with bright white window sill, drapes, rug, and sheets, very clean and very feminine. After getting dressed Trina leaves the bedroom and immediately spins around to re-enter it, grabbing her forgotten trans pass off of her dresser. She briefly glances at a picture in a small silver frame of her hugging her boyfriend of 2 years, Khalil. This time she briskly walks out of the bedroom after squirting three pushes from her perfume bottle on her way out the bedroom leaving the sent of pretty young woman in the air. She has a brief warm affectionate smirk on her face as she looks over at the couch and sees Khalil passed out in his clothes. She quickly walks over to him and kisses him on the forehead just before scooting out of the door. "Bye Baby" She says just before closing the door. Khalil is in a deep sleep while fully clothed on the couch. His cell phone starts vibrating in his pocket accompanied by a ringtone singing a song of his own creation, "Chain

Reaction". The phone sings "Chain reaction cha cha chain reaction. This is what I what I call a chain reaction" Khalil grabs the phone from his pocket without opening his eyes. He squints his eyes at the caller ID. that reads "Skrilla's Boo" and answers it.

"Mmm Hmm..."

With high heeled shoes in her purse and running shoes on her feet, Trina is in full stride on her cell phone headed one block away towards the subway entrance at Broad St. & Allegheny Ave.

"Lil, I just left for work. You better getcha ass up before your late again. I don't know why you didn't just call off. It doesn't make sense trying to do all you gotta do and work today. That's just crazy!"

"I'ma call out, I just gotta figure what I'ma tell them. I'm try'n to get it all worked out, but I got this!"

Trina responds in disbelief. "You have to be there at what 8:30? Don't you think if you're gonna call you should call kinda soon? I mean duh. Look I gotta go babe, I hear my train! Bye!"

Trina hangs up as she skips down the steps into the subway at Broad and Allegheny Ave. Khalil sits up on the couch, quickly coming back to life from a few short hours of sleep. He grabs his phone and heads to the bedroom. Unlike Trina he is slowly, yet surly coming to the realization of all he has to do for the day, and without the phone call he would most likely have been asleep for another hour or so. He walks into the bedroom and begins digging in his dresser drawer. The first sign of him living in this femininely dominated apartment is revealed, a dresser full of clothes and a closet full of sneakers. He lays his clothes across the loosely made bed and stops to collect himself, knowing there is one thing on his agenda that is highlighted in his head. He's sits at the foot of his bed prolonging for mere seconds what he knows he must do. Looking into his phone he dials his right-hand-man Lil E, and the phone begins ringing.

Lil E is already showered and dressed on the edge of his bed putting on yet another pair of new shoes on, this time a fresh pair of tan construction boots. Lil E always seems to be ahead of the game, up later and awake earlier, a true hustler poster-child. An extremely attractive young women is laying comfortably in E's bed as if it were her own, looking as if her being there was an accomplishment, she basks in the moment. He taps her leg and signals her to start getting ready while answering his phone. The dainty young beauty rises in her matching panty and bra set and looks at Lil E with a slight playful snare for ruining her moment before entering the bathroom.

"What's up my nigga?! Tonights ya night!" Lil E excitedly says into his phone.

"No nigga, today's my day! I need that bread, no more rap. I gotta-" Khalil replies with a slight degree of frustration in his voice.

"Slow down big homie. What you ain't got faith in ya boy? You know what's good. Jus gotta git with my man and I'm come'n straight at you!"

Khalil looks up at his ceiling as if he was looking through it straight into the heavens for a favor. "Yeah but what time we talk'n bout? I wanna go grab that and I'm try'n to knock it out early namsayn. Ain't no time for play'n today, you know that! I told them I was gonna pick it up early anyway." He replies reiterating its importance.

"Damn my nigga, I gotchu! Trust me. Shit, you really think I'ma let my nigga go out there looking crazy? I got this my G! You gotta git ya cut so you might as well bang that out first thing, 'for niggaz start pile'n in there. It is Friday and by the time you get a fresh boy I should be bump'n into my man. Dig me? I gotchu! Whatcha corny ass manager say about today though?"

"Oh shit! Let me call u back. Yo hit ya man. Early!" Khalil says abruptly acknowledging he has yet to call out sick. The young Women exits bathroom in cocktail dress. Lil E. looks at her in her form fitting dress and smiles, mentally patting himself on the back. Khalil hangs up the phone and scrambles through the bedroom thinking of what to tell his manager, knowing he waited until the very last minute possible and another absence could very well cost him his job. He walks into the bathroom and turns on the shower while quickly skimming thru his phone book for his co worker Kim's phone number, a young women who is secretly jealous of Khalil's girlfriend as well as the new opportunities that await him. An extremely punctual Kim is already at work at the cable company's reception desk. Kim's phone can be heard ringing from her hand bag that sits at her feet behind the desk. She takes a quick glance at the clock before diving into her purse to avoid alerting her manager. Kim's subtle instinct that Khalil was calling was confirmed by her caller ID. with his name on it. As she ever so calmly answers the phone, her tone says she has no idea who is on the other end of her line.

"Hello."

"Yo Kim I need a big favor. I…"

Kim abruptly interjects "Who Am I speaking with?"

Completely thrown off, Khalil responds. "Huh, Kim this is Khalil. I need a favor from you. Seriously I got to-"

"How did you get this number? Uh ahn… Let me find out you-"

Becoming aware of Kim's mood, an increasingly desperate Khalil interrupts her questioning. "Off the phone list Kim, besides you know I have your number cause you gave it to me when I first started, and you called me last week and asked for coffee anyway."

Doing a poor job at playing ignorant, Kim replies with a soft crush emanating from her voice.

"Oh, well you never called. I didn't know if you had it still but-"

"Come on Kimmy, why you try'n to play me? I need you to tell Ronnie I can't make it today. Matter of fact tell him I woke up sick and I tried to call but it was too early, nobody was in yet and I just woke up again".

Childishly taunting him Kim mumbles. "MmmHmmm"

"Come on Kim I got you next time you need anything. You know that. Come on, you gonna hook me up?"

"I'll tell him, but you said you got me. I know I heard that!"

"Of course! Stop trip'n you know I do. Oh shit! Kimmy did the checks come in yet? Cause I'ma definitely need that!"

Immediately knowing her favor was about to double in size, Kim lazily responds, "Yeah they over here. So whatchu gonna do?"

Khalil is now kicking himself for the added stop on his list as well as the timing of Kim's attitude. Brushing it off and pushing forward with his agenda he pleads with her to help him.

"Damn Kimmy I'm sorry I'ma need to see you on ya lunch break. Don't worry I'm gonna take care of you for this."

The cable companies manager Ronnie, a forty-six year old board certified asshole, bursts through the door and walks straight through the reception area and addresses Kim's use of her cell phone while at work, especially while at the desk. Without breaking his stride Ronnie yells out, "So this is what we do now? Take personal calls at the desk. Policy must have changed around here!"

Overhearing his manager in the background, loud and angry, in his normal disposition, Khalil seizes the moment to end the call. Whispering in his phone as if his manager could faintly hear him, he ends the call.

"Yo, shit, gotta go. I'll call you before your lunch break. 1:30 I'll hit you up! Just grab the check! Thanks Kim. You the shit! Cool." He says just before hanging up the phone.

Kim is now dancing on the borderline between feeling used and feeling useful, in and out of each emotion leaving a lingering air of confusion around her, which didn't sit well with her domineering personality. She looks at her phone with brief moment of disdain before closing it. Feeling a small degree of closure, Khalil takes the speakers from Trina's nightstand and plugs them in just over the bathroom sink and places his phone inside. While kicking his pants onto the floor, he sits his phone into the speaker dock and turns the volume up to full blast. As the beat for his song begins to pump he can hear his voice loudly bringing in the hook, "Chain reaction, cha cha Chain Reaction, now that's what the streets will call a chain reaction!" Steam fills up his bathroom mirror just in time for him to vaguely see himself in it and smile as he mouths the words to his anthem before entering the shower.

Just as the steam begins to fill Khalil's bathroom, smoke begins to pour from Lil E's nose filling his basement apartment. Blowing out a heavy, thick cloud of blunt smoke from the blunt he had lit the previous night, Lil E then mashes the remains into an astray on his coffee table. The young women returns from the bathroom with an aura of an urban supermodel, one who could easily be placed on the cover of any Hip Hop magazine or video. She is everything that she appeared to be the night before, a flawless beauty, yet as she comes out of the bathroom she quietly notices that Lil E. may not share that same authenticity. Nonetheless, she has been taken in by his confidence, just as many others have been before her.

Looking around the basement she finds herself looking at what to the naked eye would appear to be a modern bachelor pad for any young ghetto entrepreneur, yet the morning brings new revelations into the apartments band-aids. Mounted to the wall, a flat screen television directly across from his Queen size bed serves as the basements main attraction while a small glass coffee table in front of a love seat sit just a few feet way. Sitting directly under his television is a long dresser with several sneaker boxes stacked next to it displaying his collection while simulating a sneaker store. Lil E has managed to combine every room of a house into his small underground hideaway.

Always referring to the house as "my house" hiding the fact that he's a tenant in his grandmother's basement, a fact that E. sometimes forgets himself. His confidence is actually the largest and most prevalent thing in the room, so large that it has allowed him to have and exciting evening with this beauty without remembering the young starlet's name. While looking at her making her way across the basement floor he quickly realizes this is one name he wishes he had remembered.

His brief moment of gazing is abruptly shaken off before becoming completely entangled in his own fantasy. Lil E. attempts to wrap things up by standing close to the stairs leading into the fact that the day has begun and his priorities must prevail. With an agenda of her own for the day, the young women walks over and grabs his hand while forcing him into a strong moment of direct eye contact.

"Well, I had fun, if thats ok to say" she says laughing with a slight degree of embarrassment knowing their night of passion occurred just hours after they had met in a downtown bar. She looks into his eyes searching for a conformation that it was just as enjoyable for him, wanting to separate herself from the others that she knows have entered his world previously. Lil E.'s ego wouldn't allow him to confirm that he was heavily attracted to her. Being so caught up in himself, it would take him much longer than an evening to recognize the attraction. However he was fully aware that she was easily a ten in appearance and found himself struggling to remember her name, and that alone made her a notch above the rest.

With a light bulb over his head Lil E takes out his phone, "How you spell your name again? Here... You know what just program it in for me" he says asking her to store her phone number in his address book. He opens the settings to add a new contact giving her no room for any unnecessary rummaging thru his phonebook. He was sure he would be able to find out her name this way without alerting her that he didn't remember it. She unwittingly complies "Your silly. Here give me that" without knowing that E is keenly watching her store the number trying to discover her name. Killing two birds, E walks behind her and hugs her from behind trying to watch as she stores the number, unable to see from behind the curls in her hair he tells her "MmmMmmm! One more squeeze for the road."

The two share a deep hug, as Lil E. plays off an awkward moment.

"Well, alright Liiil Eeeeeee!"

"Uh...Um, Aight P.y.teeeee!" he responds escaping the moment.

The two head up the stairs into the kitchen of Lil E's grandmother's house. Emerging from basement into the row homes kitchen is the equivalent of walking from present day directly into nineteen seventy-nine, a complete contrast from Lil E's semi-modern looking basement oasis. This had gone completely unnoticed to his late night guest who had been walked in late that evening. Walking thru the outdated kitchen into a vintage looking dining room there was an undeniable atmosphere full of an of old lady's persona. It was obvious that Lil E had not purchased a China cabinet from the fifties full of old dishes and silverware. The young woman softly smiled at him as they made their way into the living room headed for the door.

Lil E's grandmother is sitting in the living room on a sofa completely covered in plastic while drinking coffee in front of her coffee table that looks like something straight from a doll house. The tiny old women is far from incoherent, although she often appeared to be off in her own world. She is well aware of her grandson's life in the fast lane and sometimes takes pleasure in giving him a few calculated jabs at his ways, though her occasional jabs are over powered by her unwavering love of her grandson. The presence of his grandmother would create a short walk of shame for the two youngsters, especially for the young woman scooting through the living room in a tight cocktail dress and high heeled shoes. Lil E. places his hand on the small of her back and attempts to slip past his grandmother without a conversation erupting.

"Morning Grandma" He says looking at the front door with extreme focus as if it were a goal line.

"Mmmm" She responds without dignifying him with a verbal response.

Letting out another warm smile E's company turns and softly mouths "Hello" while maintaining a constant motion towards the door.

"Mmmhmmm" she says without looking at the two, keeping her eyes glued to the news channel on her television.

Just as Lil E touches the knob and cracks the door a jab is thrown.

"Aren't you going to introduce me to your new girlfriend? Would seem like the right thing to do." She says without even looking in their direction, the perfect blend of a caring older woman and a devious old lady. It was obvious to Lil E that he had yet again walked into another perfectly timed punch as he often does. Knowing his grandmother had no interest in meeting his new friend. He looked at her begging for sympathy by way of telepathy. Making a split second executive decision he grabs her hand leading her out the door.

"Sorry Grandma we're in a little bit of a rush this morning, but don't worry you'll be seeing more of her real soon."

Feeling extremely uncomfortable in her dress but unwilling to ignore the request for an introduction, she pulls her hand away and gently extends it towards the old woman.

"I'm sorry. This is rude of him. I'm Maria."

"Well..alright Darlin'." She says showing her respect for being acknowledged, and restoring Maria's dignity before leaving.

"Boy you be careful out there now."

Before leaving he smiles partly at his grandmother and partly at the fact that he now knows his mystery dates name.

13

The sun was now directly in the faces of the two as a beautiful day in North Philly had officially commenced.

"My bad, It's just you let her get started and she'll have you in there the whole dizzay."

"Yeah they'll do that sometimes. Call me ok."

"No doubt!"

She leans in and kisses him on the cheek before stepping down to the pavement. She crosses the street and gets into a new Malibu parked directly across the street. Lil E follows getting into an old yet extremely clean Chevy Caprice classic with a shiny set of rims forcing the car about a foot higher into the air than normal.

"Shit!" he mouthed to himself while staring at the gas light highlighting his dashboard after starting the car. Lil E's classic wheels was on beyond empty. He knew the first place he was headed was the gas station but the longer he had his engine running it would become a question if he would even make it there. He looks over to Maria waiting for her to pull off so he could shut his engine off and preserve the last few drops of gas in his tank. With an awkward smile, he says while clenching his teeth "Can you hurry ya pretty lil ass up." She smiles back at him in return and begins to pull out of the parking space. Lil E. fiddles with radio stalling his pulling off. After changing the station to or three times he looks to his left again only see her smiling as she harshly turns her wheel to keep inching out of the spot. Turning the wheel as if trying to reverse an ocean liner, she backs her rear wheel onto the curb trying to exit a space that could fit one and a half of her cars. In what is taking far above the average time, each second begins to feel like an eternity for Lil E as he stares at his dashboard, only able to see the gas light that appeared to be staring back at him.

"Damn. You can back ya ass up but can't back that lil ass car up. Come ooon shorty!" Finally wiggling her way out of the parking spot she pulls out and heads down the street.

Lil E watches as her car pulls to the corner and turns out of view immediately shutting his engine off. He picks up his phone and lowers the radio while calling another young street entrepreneur who owes him a substantial amount of money, twelve hundred dollars to be exact, that he in turn owes to his best friend Khalil, who is in desperate need of the money. The phone begins ringing and E immediately fills with pressure as each ring starts to feel like another small eternity. The call reaches the seventh ring and is finally answered.

"Yo!" E's associate says, calmly answering the phone.

"Yo, yo...damn What's good?!"

"What's good my G? I got you. Everything, everything? It's still early as shit, but I'm out here my G!" He says reaffirming that everything is on schedule.

"Nah fam, I need that thing a.s.a.p.! I can't let it get all late in the day. You feel me? I told you that's not even for me! That's for my peoples! So-"

"You trip'n, I already got you on me, I just gotta bump into you. It's still early as shit, but I'm out here already. I'm on the way over your side. I mean if you wanna come on over here and meet me real quick you could do that too, but I'm make'n my way over their now G."

Lil E. turns the key and takes a hard look at the gas light staring him in the face again.

"Sheeeeeiiit... I'm say'n you already on the way over here right? Aight just make sure you git wit me. I gotta get that to my nigga asap! He needs that shit on some real shit namsay'n." he says agreeing to wait for his associate to meet him on his side of the neighborhood.

"I already know what it is. I'm come'n over there. I'ma hit you up soon as I get on your side my G!"

"Aight Fam, but on the early side!"

"Fa shiggidy! E, I gotchu! One."

"One!" Lil E says before hanging up the phone and stepping out of his car onto the narrow North Philly sidewalk.

# Chapter Two

J ust as Lil E's boot hits the pavement, four blocks over on Cumberland St. the boot of Terrence, a neighborhood barber touches the ground just outside his barbershop. Terrence hops out of an extremely clean, conservative SUV and heads toward his shop. Crossing the street he looks at the sign hovering above the shop's grate that reads "Faded". It would seem that every time he looked at the sign it would force him into a moment of introspection, reflecting on his journey into the ownership of the shop.

"Morning Ms. Gloria How the kids?" He says to a woman passing by. The woman smiles just as bright as the day and responds "They're fine...looking to put me in an early grave as all." She says jokingly. Terrence laughs off her comment as she moves along.

"Shit!" he quietly mumbles to himself realizing he's left his shop keys in his truck. He quickly shuffles across the street to grab his keys and notices Khalil a few houses down approaching the shop. The sound of a loud car system can be heard nearing the corner.

Terrence walks back across the street greeting Khalil outside.

"Skrilla Kay, Skrilla Kay!"

"Big T what's the deal?"

Before a conversation could be evoked the two were interrupted by an extremely loud and muffled bass coming from a freshly washed, burgundy late model pickup truck with a gleaming pair of 26" rims that had just pulled up to the corner. The midnight colored tint of the truck window rolls down and reveals the driver, Big Chollie, a North Philly certified hustler and fixture in the neighborhood. Although he was known by the entire neighborhood as a fierce drug dealer, he had previously managed to surpass the corner level of dealing, and in the Badlands this qualified him for the right to play his music as loud and obnoxiously as he chose. Looking at him from the outside looking in, it wasn't a question of when is he gonna grow up, it was more of a "He's grown up to be a drug dealer" aura that he possessed. This was a hard thing to remove, so he in turn embraced it and wore it like a tattoo.

Big Chollie's reputation was as loud as his radio, exuding all aspects of the stereotypes that have been attached to his neighborhood existence. The two look towards the truck window and Big Chollie and Terrence exchange a silent nod exhibiting a mutual respect for one another. Just a few years had passed since the severance of their partnership in a minor empire that had been constructed in their twenties. There remained a slight undercurrent of admiration on behalf of both of the young gentleman. Although years had gone by, Terrence walking away from what they'd built would never fully register to Chollie. His admiration stemmed from knowing that Terrence could be just as successful in the street if he chose to and couldn't be a hundred percent sure that he could manage to pull of Terrence's new lifestyle had he chose to do so. The streets had inadvertently become an ethnicity to him, something that could not be removed and would always be the first thing people would see.

For Terrence it was much simpler due to the far unequal balance of admiration that he would share. He would merely find himself in moderate awe that Big Chollie had maintained a life that he was sure would expire at any moment. Dumping his profits from their previous business into his barbershop that was now profitable, had garnered him an equal yet very different type of respect in the streets.

The frame of Big Chollie's glasses catches the sun and reflects it into the face of anyone looking at him. Quite similar to the frame that borders Terrence's sign above his barber shop entrance. Their life choices had driven them worlds apart, yet the nods exchanged would signify an acknowledgment of their past.

"Skrillz! What's good witchu pimp'n? You thow'n it down tonight right?! You know you gotta rep for the hood. These lil niggaz count'n on you Dog" Chollie says after lowering his music.

Khalil notices an older man getting out of his car and heading towards the shop but is unwilling to refuse Big Chollie's conversation. He walks to the truck with a smile taking up half of his face and diplomatically shakes Chollie's hand.

"No digitty! I'ma hold it down. I got some heat. You know I'ma turn it up out there! You gone be in there right?"

"Sheeeeeiiit, that ain't my thing. Ya'll sold out anyway right?"

"Yeah they been sold out. But shit, I might be able to work something out. Namsay'n?"

Knowing he had enough pull in the city to enter the sold out venue if he chose to, Big Chollie chuckles and responds. "I'm good lil nigga, but thanks for the gesture. My lil young thing works down there. Matter fact she said y'all niggaz was gone be on the big screen, fuck'n jumbo tron n'shit. You blow'n up Lil nigga!"

Noticing that the old man was now standing outside of the shop, Skrilla became quickly aware that his conversation with Big Chollie was an expensive one, costing him the first haircut of the day. With cars backing up behind the truck on the narrow North Philly block, Skrilla takes his opportunity.

"Ah..My Man! Damn, let me get over here in this shop, 'for I be on the big screen looking like this! You feel me? Aight Big Chollie!" He says shaking his hand and pulling away towards the shop.

"Aight young'n do ya thing." Mouths Big Chollie while returning the music's volume to its normal obscene level and pulling off while taking one more glance at Faded's coveted sign in his rearview.

Skrilla walked towards the shop continuing to greet Terrence who was fiddling with his keys in the padlock on the grate covering the entrance of the barbershop.

"What's up wit the whats up?! Figured I'd come get out here early, feel me?"

"Aww shit Skrillz! What I'ma celebrity barber now? A fuck'n stylist?! It's on huh? The stadium! Thats the big leagues baby!" Terrence replied in attempts to boost the esteem of the young mc.

"Man hear you go! I'm just the opening act. This ain't no big leagues." A humbled Skrilla responds.

"The opening act for the muthafuck'n Career Criminals! Shit! Whatever it is, it's an opportunity to do more. Let me be twenty-one over again, shiiit!"

Terrence didn't elaborate on what he meant by doing more but it was subtly evident what he was referring to with Big Chollie pulling off into a life of crime and him staying behind and opening the doors if his shop. The fourteen year gap in age between Terrence and Skrilla made Skrilla subliminally store the messages he was given. Unfortunately, he was too young to know that he should apply them immediately. Terrence knew and understood this, yet the fact that Skrilla was willing to store the messages raised him above more than half of the neighborhood in his eyes. The grate flew up and the three generations of men filed into the shop.

Just over five short North Philadelphia blocks away, on Germantown Avenue in the neighborhoods shopping district another grate was also being lifted. This one was that of a small jewelry store in the middle of the avenue, surrounded by over priced junk retailers selling off brand products to anyone who was unwilling to leave the neighborhood.

Lacking the esthetic beauty of the barbershop's sign, the jewelry store donned a wooden sign that had been repainted twice before that read "The Jewelry Box". It was the entrepreneurial vision of the store's two Russian owners. Eli, who had just unlocked the door of the padlock on the grate of their American dream, was stopped from entering the shop by the sound of a man selling CDs and DVDs along the avenue sidewalk. Although this would occur every day, today he stopped in frustration.

Nearing the jewelry store the DVD man adds an air of life and character to the block as the store owners open their doors to begin their Friday, which was easily the most profitable day for all of them. He saw himself as a business owner himself, no different from the others which enabled him to fraternize with the other owners with confidence as he lugged a duffel bag full of copyright infringement up the avenue.

Pulling into a parking spot directly in front of the jewelry store, Eli's partner Mark parks a white Mercedes that is in desperate need of a car wash. Exiting his car in his normal energetic fashion Mark steps out just as the DVD man reaches the store.

"Big bag! Big bag! I got movies by the tons! I got comedies! I got dramas! And those shaky bun buns! Check out some movies today fellas?"

In a heavy Russian accent Eli replies with his frustrations spilling over. "Not today my friend! I can't have you out here scaring away my customers. This is place of business. Not for you to do this nonsense."

An ambulance siren blares down the street towards Temple hospital which was several blocks away and also on Germantown Avenue. The sound of an apartment window opening just above the jewelry stores sign had been drowned out by the blare. A rather short and timid Chinese man Mr. Jung, the building's owner, peers down on the conversation with a look of disdain bubbling inside of him while letting out a heavy breath that had also gone unnoticed due the siren.

"I'm not try'n to steal your business Brotha, just try'n to make one of my own. You feel me? Y'all good brothas can understand that!" the DVD man says looking at Eli.

"Not today! We have no time for this! Move this from here, you must go!"

After quickly feeding a parking meter Mark adds "Yes, you must go from here. This is a business. We do not do this here."

Placing business back at the forefront the young salesman recognized Mark as a customer and then smiles with a wide grin.

"Oh shit, I got what you want! Round Black Booty 3. I just got it in! Bam!" He says shuffling thru his bag and pulling out a pornographic DVD covered with black woman.

"Nonsense! You must move away from here with this garbage. This is not decent. Move from here!"

"What is you talk'n bout I just sold you one and two the other day! Y'all trip'n out here, on this fine Friday morning too." He says attempting to lighten the mood.

Staring at the DVD, an extremely embarrassed Mark spouts out "The police will come here! You see!" referring to the siren and pointing at the ambulance that had just passed by.

"Police? Man y'all trip'n for real! I'm out. I'll see y'all tomorrow Fellas."

Blasting off as he stepped into the street to cross it, the young hustler hollers. "Big bag! Big bag! I got movies by the tons! I got comedies! I got dramas! And those shaky bun buns!"

With the DVD man's back to them, Mark looks at Eli with a shameful smirk that says, "I'm caught red handed, So what?!".

Eli shakes his head at Mark as the two enter the store. Immediately after the store's door closes with the owners now inside Mr. Jung firmly closes the window above the store after witnessing to the conversation.

Mr. Jung turns around after shutting the window only to find his very pregnant wife, mother in law, and five year old twins staring him directly in the face. The family was nestled in this cramped apartment for several years now and had now out grown the apartment physically as well as mentally. The apartment bared no decor, and no design, just empty white walls painted with grease spots from heavy cooking in the tiny quarters. A foot tall Buddha statue next to a bowl of fruit sitting in the corner served as the only decorative piece they had amongst them. Mr. Jung remained under constant scrutiny from his wife while under the watchful eyes of her mother. He points at the children's coloring book on their tiny kitchen table, forcing his son and daughter's eyes off of him. Mrs. Jung steps away from a large pot of vegetables stewing on stove while her mother posts at an ironing board in the living room that also served as a dining room and kitchen.

Breaking the silence, Mrs. Jung looks at him and loudly spats. "You know today is rent day! They have store! They have money! Today they must pay! No excuses!"

"I know what today is! Let me handle this! I will take care of those two."

Cutting no slack, she quickly replies. "You've been handling this every month and every month they pay late! One month almost no pay! We tired of this Ramsung Tv with Fose speaka! Your children play with Gamestation 5! We need real things! They must pay!"

"You just calm down and let me deal with store!" He says firmly trying to restore control without allowing his voice to near the volume of hers.

Mr. Jung storms off through the living room assuring himself the last word, passing his mother in law who was ironing slow and steady while cutting her eyes at him on his way into the bathroom. The old woman reached into a laundry basket lined with a laundry bag and pulled out another wrinkled dollar bill and began ironing it, slow and steady. He could feel her eyes on him as he moved through their cramped apartment. Crossing the bathroom's threshold, just before the door closes Mr. Jung hears his wife yell one last time "Today!". He leans on his miniature sink and looks into his rickety medicine cabinet mirror and pleads. "Why?!?"

# Chapter Three

Downstairs in the Jewelry Box preparations for the day begin inside one of the avenues highlighted businesses. Lined with extremely cheap products being purchased along the very same block, everything on this street seems to resemble modern looking junk. The shop's showcase is a few fat women's leans from falling over, yet surprisingly beneath the cabinets are filled with very expensive, quality jewelry.

Mark and Eli have become more of magicians than the capitalist they believe they are, mastering the art of illusion. They have quite successfully impressed upon the avenue that they are the owners of this very prestigious environment and that it is something to be admired.

Mark dashes into the store fashioning his belt, coming from the bathroom in the shop's back office and heading for the showcase with a crisp Forbes magazine under his arm. Letting out a loud belch, Mark chuckles and loudly boast "Whew! All that coffee, has to come out right? What goes in must come out!" He says jokingly. Having his comment ignored by his partner he throws the magazine on top of a wrinkled pile of the previous months editions. It had become a habit for him to read while using the restroom upon his daily arrival. He was now averaging four to five sentences per day which was enough for him to consider himself an avid reader, well informed of his entrepreneurial requirements.

Eli now has cases of jewelry on top of the counter and has begun filling the showcase. Placing a tray of diamond rings into the show case, one catches his eye with a twinkle. For a split second it was as if the diamond had looked back at him by way of a gentle sparkle.

Waisting no time, Mark's greatly agitated partner erupts.

"This is bullshit! We shouldn't be living like this! Two business men like us should have better problems than this. Shit, you and I should own half of this neighborhood by now!"

Feeling the need to reassure him, Mark replies with confidence. "We will! Can't you see we are on the verge of something big here! This store here is just the beginning. Remember, look how far we've come! This country is ours for the taking my friend. We just have to start here, with this one store."

"And how in the hell are we going to do that?! We have bills piling up. This is an embarrassment!"

"Where is your vision? This is America! At any moment we could make millions! This is land of opportunity and were standing in it!"

"Vision? Let me tell you about vision! I vision landlord coming downstairs for rent. I see us with no store, no money, standing directly on this land of opportunity. That's what I see. I also see a pile of bills on this table!"

"If you've got heartbeat you can prosper. That is the way. Same way in Russia, but here is much faster. There is millions of dollars just outside that door."

"No, there is junkies and drug dealers outside that door! We need a store downtown. This is North Philadelphia! What's wrong with the phone? What is this?!" Eli says while harshly smacking to stores phone desperately searching for a dial tone.

"Minor set back. That phone is off because I needed to pay this cell phone bill. Yesterday I payed some bills remember?"

"Yes, I remember! There was money for the phone, the electric, and the gas! What is your cell phone doing in that?! We have no business phone so you can talk to your women?!"

With a confident chuckle Mark replies. "Calm down my friend, everything is under control. The money for the gas, I used some on the electric, and the water was extra because someone leave the toilet running for I don't know what? So, I used some of the electrics money. And the money for the phone, that was a business decision."

"Business? What business!?"

"The kid is coming in today!" Mark says completely confusing Eli.

"What!?"

"The rap star, he's coming for his chain today! What are you thinking about?"

Boiling over, Eli slams the phone down and shouts, "So you figure it is better if we have no phone if he calls us?!"

Sensing his undeniable anger, Mark responds in a much calmer voice.

"It was three months ago he started paying for that chain. And you don't remember but our phone was off then when he came in for down payment. So I give him my cell phone number instead. Don't worry I'm on top of everything."

Mark rapidly punches in the safes combination and opens the door. In utter disbelief, Eli looks and stares at him and with a syne voice of humor fires back, "So let me get this right, yesterday we had money for bills. Today we have no money and we owe on all our bills?! And worse, today is rent day! Not to mention we must also pay the girl! And your on top of things?"

Mark reaches into the safe and delicately pulls out it's only contents, a gleaming white gold chain with a diamond filled pendant in shape of an S with a crown on top glistening under the stores lights. He places it on a soft cloth as he looks at Eli and smiles.

"Don't worry my friend, the money has been in the safe all along!"

"My God! You've gone mad. I'm going for coffee. Give me money." Eli says motioning his hand for some money from the store's register.

Mark opens the register and reality quickly sets in while looking into an almost empty drawer. He takes four one dollar bills from it leaving a remaining dollar and some loose change in the register. This was done at light speed trying to avoid grabbing Eli's attention, as well as letting the reality of this empty drawer effect his spirits. He passes him the money as if there were thousands more where that came from and Eli immediately brushes out the door.

"I'm leaving! Come lock the door behind me."

Mark closes the door and reaches into his pocket pulling out a pack of cigarettes. He takes one from the pack and starts smacking the filter onto the showcase glass. Staring into the cluster of diamonds in Skrilla's pendant he mouths "Where are you kid?".

# Chapter Four

On a tiny yet heavy populated Sterner Street, a block neatly tucked next to Lehigh Avenue, it appeared to be much later in the day than it actually was. The block was dominated by a Puerto Rican presence that resonated throughout the street. Flags of the island, bumper stickers and more were boisterously posted on everything from windows and mailboxes to license plates and steering wheel covers up and down the street.

With twenty-five houses on each side of the small street it would give residency to almost two hundred people on this one block. Half of the street was lined with cars with two wheels in the street and two on the sidewalk. This was the only way cars would be able to be parked and allow traffic to flow through the narrow street.

Directly in the middle of the street inside of a pink painted row, the Gonzalez family swallows the living room almost busting it at the seams. The house was decorated with photos of immediate and extended family and a few plants. The furniture on the other hand was not exactly desirable due to the near one thousand pounds of family members being planted on it daily.

Ms. Gonzalez and a young Mita are sitting squarely on the sofa equaling five hundred and fifty pounds of women power, while another three hundred and fifty pounds that makes up Mr. Gonzalez is leaning back in a recliner with a plate of fried plantains resting on his stomach. The family's kitchen is blocked off by a play pen occupied by two children ages one and two playing as loudly as they possibly can between glances at the living room television.

Footsteps from the upstairs can be heard over the sound of the Latin soap operas playing on the tv, which was an obvious spectacle, being seventy inches big in this tiny North Philly row. Just as the footsteps reach the top steps to come down the stairs Ms. Gonzalez yells up. "Oh no you don't Jessica, you better wake your brother's lazy ass up before you leave!" as if she could see through the ceiling into the upstairs.

"Ahh Ma, I gotta go!" Jessica says before turning around and heading down the hall.     She starts banging on her brother's door with an open palm and shouting, "Manny, Manny, Manny get up! Ma said!"

She turns around without waiting for an answer feeling that mission was complete and shuffles down the stairs. Down comes two legs the color of twenty-four carrot gold attached to what could easily be referred to as "Ms. Puerto Rico" of North Philadelphia that is. Jessica brushes through the living room as fast as possible with full make up and large gold earrings and a tiny pair of shorts.

Passing the stairs, she leans over and kisses her nephews. "Bye babies, love you!" "Bye Mami, Bye Mita." she says while headed to her father and trying to avoid another chore from the two who were staring at her legs wishing they could screw them off of her and put them on themselves. She leans over and kisses her father on the forehead. "Bye Pa"

"Bye bye Jessita. Be careful." He said, quietly mumbling the only words he had spoken all day.

Directly on her front steps Jessica gasps, feeling like she had just escaped Alcatraz. She pulled a large keychain from the inside of her small clutch to lock her door, absolutely certain that no one was going to get up from their sunken seats to do so. The sun beams in her face reflecting off of her earrings and gold colored chain that made up the shoulder strap of her purse. Stepping off of her steps in a powder white pair of sneakers, Jessica looks to her left into her neighbors house noticing her young neighbor waiting for her.

"When we get'n married?" Her ten year old neighbor slickly says to her with impeccable timing. She quickly looks at him leaning in his doorway topless in a pair of baggy jeans shorts with his boxers showing and flip-flops on his feet.

"Ten more years Papi!" She says smiling with a subtle flirt as she heads up the block with her hips swinging unconsciously from left to right like a pendulum. Passing a small bodega on her corner Jessica blows a kiss at an old man sweeping the pavement, lighting up his every morning. And every morning the old man was reeled back in by the eyes of his wife calling him back into the store. Turning off of Lehigh onto Germantown ave, she was now just two blocks away from work and almost ten minutes late.

She began the short stretch to her job when a car slows down in traffic and taps the horn at her. A young man in a sweaty tank top shirt sticks his head out of the window and yells. "What's up Mami? Let me give you a ride. Your way too beautiful to be walking! Let me give you a ride Mama!"

The inside of his car appeared to be hotter than it was outside, but this wouldn't stop any healthy young man in his position from attempting to date a young Ms. Puerto Rico of North Philly now would it?

"No Thank you Papi, I'm just going right up here. Thank you" Jessica says looking at him and politely smiling while declining the ride.

"Its cool, hop in. I'll drive you to the moon if I have to."

Their would be conversation was abruptly interrupted by the sound of his car crunching the bumper of the car in front of him that was stopped at a stop sign. The driver's door flies open and out pops an angry women headed straight for the damage. He has one eye on her looking at the bumper and the other watches Jessica's hips swinging up the avenue turning every head on the street as she walks by. He was left torn between crying for this young beauty walking away giggling at his expense, or the fact that he has no license or insurance and is at the seen of an accident that he's caused.

Finally reaching the Jewelry Box, Jessica taps on the glass with her ring signaling Mark to open the door. He comes from behind the counter with a wide smile to open the door. She walks into the store and before anything else she immediately notices two cups of coffee at each end of the showcase.

"Aww…Did I miss coffee again? Seem like no matter what time I come in I just missed a cup."

"We didn't know if you were coming in today? You didn't call so we had no way of knowing." Mark says while thinking of the empty register and the paycheck that they don't yet have for her. With a natural cheerfulness she spouts. "Seeing me here everyday isn't proof enough?! Anyway, why don't we just go next door and buy a coffee maker? It's only like 20 bucks."

Eli, who isn't in the best of moods and severely lacks poise says with an angry tone, "Today is Friday. We have to get ready to sell, sell, sell! We cannot be concerned with coffee pots and toys. We are here for doing business!"

"Toys? This guy is trip'n. What's he talk'n bout? Toys? Wow!"

Mark instinctively leaps into diffuse Eli's comment, which was delivered with the grace of a breakdancer in a glass wear shop with the lights off.

"What he means is let's see what we sell today. Maybe we can get expresso maker instead? Yes?"

Jessica roles her eyes at the both of them and grabs the glass cleaner to wipe down the showcases. While polishing she sees a man in his early twenties with his hand on the door and tells Mark to hit the buzzer to unlock the door.

The young customers steps into the store amidst all of sparkling jewelry and bypasses it all starring directly into Jessica's cleavage.

"Hello, can I help you with something?" She says to him softly.

Her voice simply wasn't enough to move his eyes. He gazed into her chest and said. "Yeah I was wondering if I could-" His sentence was chopped in half by an understandably rude Eli who was fed up at watching him watching her. "She doesn't like you! She will not give time of day. Unless you buy the watch."

"I might want the watch. Shit, How you know I don't want the watch?" The customer says cockily after being snatched out of his stupor and trying to avoid being embarrassed in front of the neighborhood beauty. "Ha! Watch? What watch you want? You want to watch this pretty young girl walking around your bedroom. That's what you want to watch. Not gonna happen Buddy!"

Jessica smiles at Eli's comment, partly feeling he was defending her and partly finding the whole situation amusing. The customer sucks his teeth and backs up to leave the store trying to avoid eye contact with any of them. Backing all the way up to the door he is met with a buzz and exists the store. The door closes behind him and Jessica looks at the two in amazement.

"Your crazy! How do you know what he wants? He might have bought the whole store? You never know Papi. That's why I'm nice to all of them. Its better that way."

"She's right my friend. We must listen to her about these things. This is her neighborhood. She understands the people." Mark adds.

"I understand the people just fine. What you think I don't know this? Its simple, watch. What's good with you? What's the business homie? What's pop'n? We are crackers, you are Mami, and this is not gold its bling. What else is there to know?"

"Very cute...Ooh buzz the door!" Jessica says spotting another customer at the door.

Mark buzzes the door and this time in walks an old women with glasses that had lenses almost a half an inch thick pressing into her cheekbones. Throughout the Jewelry Box's time on the avenue the three had developed a six sense of who wanted what, and it was extremely evident to them that she was one of the day's many browsers. Treating her no differently than any other customer, Jessica smiles and greets her as she enters the store.

"Hi, can I help you with something?"

"Oh I was just looking. I haven't seen this store before and I've lived here since '63. Just wanted to see what you had in here as all. Well, that's pretty. What's that one cost?" She says pointing at a diamond encrusted ring.

Jessica reaches into the case of rings to pull back the tag while she reluctantly says, "That one is $3500 but we could probably bring it down some. Would you like to try it on?"

"Goodness no! That's almost more than I paid for my house. You people must be swimming in money. The good life huh?" She says in complete awe while smiling and taking another glance at the ring.

"No Mam, just living normal. Maybe the people that buy it live the good life, but we're here working Ma." Jessica humbly replies while chuckling.

"Oh I can certainly understand that. Well, let me go now. I could have a heart attack just look'n at these prices. Goodness, I know I'm scared to find out, but what does something like that cost?" she says while peering behind the showcase to the cloth with Skrilla's chain lying on it, revealing that her eye site is far more keen than her glasses let on.

Jessica looks over her shoulder to see what the women was referring to and notices Skrilla's chain. Her face came alive as if she had seen a long lost friend. "Oh yeah, that was $8500."

"Oh, now I know I'm in the wrong place! I knew I was afraid to ask. You folks let me go on now." The woman stated sensing a widening generational gap amongst them. Headed for the door she is stopped in her tracks by Jessica laughing in agreement and saying, "Don't worry that one is sold already.

"Somebody done bought that one already? That great big thing right there?"

"Almost Mama, just a little bit left to go."

"Wait now somebody's make'n payments? Like house payments on a necklace?"

Jessica smiles and shrugs off the comment as the woman heads for the door.

"Now I know I done heard it all. Good Day to y'all" She says just before opening the door and stepping onto the increasingly hot pavement. Jessica turns around singing "Chain reaction, cha cha chain reaction" while carefully picking up Skrilla's chain that she hadn't noticed was out of the safe.

"Oh yeah, what time is he coming to pick this up?" She says holding the chain in front of her. Leaning on the counter with his arms folded Eli adds.

"If he comes today!"

"Nah he's coming. They gotta show tonight! He's opening up for the Career Criminals tonight! Unless he got another chain already, he's coming for this. Oh my god, where y'all been at?! He gotta song about it and everything. Y'all bug'n!"

"You see, he will be here! It is still early, yes." Mark confidently chimes in after soaking in the new information.

"What time Am I getting payed to today? Cause I'm hungry, and I'm broke. Plus my brother needs to borrow some money and I ain't about to have that crazy fool keep bothering me. That's for damn sure." She asserts.

Seizing the opportunity to have an irrefutable point, Eli looks at the two of them and says, "So you are late and you want to be payed early? America is great place." Mark silently cosigns him, once again reflecting on the empty register.

"You've gotta be kidding me?" Jessica says, speaking to both of the as if they were just one person, who happened to be full of shit.

Meanwhile, back at the cable company business as usual is not business as usual. The company seems to be operating a step behind in the days agenda making Khalil present even in his absence.

"Where in the hell is that damn Armstrong?" Ronnie screams at two of the cable company's drivers on their way out of the building.

"Who, who?"

"That Khalil, or Skrilla, or whatever his god damn name is! Where the fuck is he?!" Ronnie yells throughout the office, resonating in the earshot of the staff and customers as well. Kim purposely had waited until the last possible moment to let him know of Skrilla's absence and nonchalantly responds to her raging boss.

"Oh I forgot, he's sick he said he can't come in."

"Sick huh? Ain't this some bullshit!" He says, now with Kim locked in his eyesight sitting comfortably at the reception desk. Kim leans on the desk pulling on a piece of gum that she is rapidly chewing.

"Nah he called in earlier, he's sick for real. He probably even gonna miss his lil show tonight too." She slips into the conversation purely out of jealousy.

"What lil show? What in the hell is go'n on around here?!!?"

"Ain't nothin'. He was supposed to be performing down at the stadium tonight that's all. You know he raps." Kim uttered, firmly planting herself evenly on both sides of the fence siding with her manager as well as keeping her commitment to Skrilla.

"Oh I get it! He can go'n play superstar while we go to work and handle his shit huh? Is that how the game works?!?"

# Chapter Five

The morning has now officially dissipated and the heat has quickly risen to a hot and sticky status. Inside the barber shop is quite the opposite. A cool breeze from Terrence's central air unit is calm and steady, just as his hand is on the razor making one last scrape on the older mans face. Skrilla, along with two others remain patiently waiting in the wings for their turn in the chair. Terrence heads to the sink and turns it on allowing the water to heat up, drawing a full steam over the sink. He places a fresh white towel under the water as Skrilla begins to steam up just as fast as the water.

Before he completely bubbles over he notices Lil E strolling up outside the shop window smoking like a steam train, donning a haircut he had gotten the previous day. Skrilla immediately hits the door before Lil E enters the shop.

"Yo T. I'm outside" he says before exiting.

"Don't go nowhere we finishing up now."

Skrilla could almost sense that E hadn't yet picked up the money as he steps out of the shop and shakes his hand. He sighs and then blurts out at E.

"What's good wit you?"

Lil E, with his normal nonchalant attitude smirks and happily responds. "What's up what's up! What's good witchu? Damn. You still ain't get a cut. What the fuck? Thought you came out here early. My nigga on some cool shit, huh?"

"Nah man...Ol' head got here first, I'm next. He think he at the crib or some shit. He want his nose hairs, ear hairs done, damn! But what's good? You seen ya man?"

E extends the blunt he is smoking to Skrilla who refuses the spliff and quickly looks at him sideways.

"Nah, not yet. He on the way over here now. Chillax my nigga! I know it been a minute but I gotchu today! Real rap! Just chill. Everything's gonna be smooth. Shit, its go'n to be on tonight homie, bitches galore!"

Skrilla's face screws up as he stands back and looks at his friend.

"Yo this ain't a game! I need that shit and you over here talking bout bitches. Come on man that's fucked up!"

"Whatchu talk'n bout? I told you my man was on his way, chill homie, he's come'n. Tonight we up in there you diggy!"

"Yeah I dig. But ya man gotta hurry the fuck up, fa real though. All I'm wait'n on is you Fam! Dig dat?!"

Terrence taps on the window signaling Skrilla into the shop just as Lil E's phone rings. The older man walks out of the shop through the marijuana filled air while E tries vigorously not to exhale. The old man passes and greets them in doing so.

"How u gentlemen doing?"

"Fine Sir" E. says with a cloud of smoke pouring out of his mouth. The man shakes his head and continues on his way. Skrilla skips back into the shop while Lil E hangs back and answers his ringing phone.

"Yo, what's pop'n? Aight, aight thats cool. That'll work! We here…at the shop. One!"

Stepping into the shop Lil E walks past a few empty chairs lined along the wall for customers and plops into an empty barber chair as if he owns the place. Terrence pays him no mind as he places the cape around Skrilla's neck before grabbing his clippers. The radio is playing accompanied by a muted tv mounted on the wall. Terrence dives right into the haircut knowing exactly how he wants it and decides to pick Skrilla's brain in the process.

"Skrilla Kay! What it is my man?"

"Shit I can't call it! What's go'n on wit you? Everything everything?"

"Yeah Man, business is business. That's what I hope you keep ya mind on."

"Oh you know that! That's what comes first."

"Yeah I hear you but you got this mutherfucka wit you that's why I'm asking you. Ol' Easy Street E over here. He says nodding his head towards E. slouched in the chair.

"Ah man hear you go again hate'n on the kid! Chill wit all that man." E. says in a cool monotone voice jumping at the chance to defend himself and being too young to realize he had just bitten into the bait, hook, line and sinker.

Terrence smiles and pauses from straightening out Skrilla's hairline.

"Hate'n? Don't even try that wit me Lil nigga! You got to make sense around here! How am I hate'n on you? What you got that I want? I know your young ass think you still got a chance to take over the world, right? This ain't about hate'n! This is about having something to do with your life and not fucking it up! That's what it's about. This ya man right?"

"50 grand! You know that!"

"Well, remember that! Be his man then! Don't be that nigga that don't know all he's waiting to do is fuck something up! Fuck'n groupies is not a job mutha-fucka!"

"Tell em again ah!" Skrilla says laughing as he jumps in cosigning his barber. E quietly spins the chair feeling the tension between he and Terrence building. He figured that his clothes and style gave him immunity from such conversations and didn't understand what it was that Terrence saw in him that he didn't like. He stared into his phone playing off the comments allowing them to go in one ear and right out the other while trying to keep his cool. What bothered him the most was not knowing exactly what it was that Terrence saw that had him pinned as full of shit.

Before there was a chance for the silence to mount, the music on the radio is interrupted by the stations Dj who has an important announcement.

"Aww shit!! Turn the radio up y'all" E says hanging on to the radios every word. Terrence stops the cut and points the remote at his stereo turning up the volume. The Dj blasts off in a hyped up radio voice.

"Tonight it's going all the way down! The "Career Criminals" will be shutting the Stadium down ya'll! The sold out concert is tonight! Also you know we can't forget North Philly's own Skrilla Kay will be performing live! This is gonna be a BIG look for him! Matter of fact Skrilla if you out there, hit us up on the lines homie!"

Lil E. Jumps out of the chair and slaps the hand of one of the waiting customers.

"Aw shit nigga! My nigga is blow'n up! Hit them niggaz up and let em know what it is. We take'n over! Yeah!"

Terrence cuts his eyes at him knowing he is overly excited at playing the role of the sidekick, a trait that just didn't sit well with him, genuinely wanting to see Skrilla succeed. E wouldn't notice the look due to him now pacing the shop waiting for Skrilla to get thru on the station.

Skrilla pulls out his phone and dials a private line he has to the radio allowing him to be connected after a few rings.

"Yo yo it's skrillz...Aight." He says to the operator waiting to be put on air.

Terrence brushes the hair out of his clippers and the shop here's the Dj announce his presence.

"Now here's a man on his job ladies and gentlemen. Skrilla Kay is on the line listeners! Skrilla what's go'n on baby talk to me?!"

"Aw man you know we definitely in the building tonight! Philly is in for a real treat. I'ma be put'n in some work on that stage and you know the Career Criminals go'n to kill it for sho. Shout out to them! Yeah tonight we definitely out to prove to the city the movement is real. So shout out to everybody coming out tonight! Let's do this!" Skrilla says with the poise and diplomacy of a true artist.

Terrence pauses with a proud look that is quickly broken by glancing at Lil E. rubbing his hands together as if he was ready to start an empire at that instant. The Dj continues on with his radio blast at the city's full attention, much less the entire shop was quietly on the edge of their seats watching Hip Hop history commence.

"You heard it here first y'all. So let me ask you will the infamous S. Chain be with you?"

"Oh it's only right!" Skrilla says confidently knowing the entire tristate was listening.

"Aight Baby…tonight!"

"Oh, real quick let me shout out my man Terrence over here at Faded Barbershop get'n me fresh for the night ya dig!"

The Dj without having a clue who Terrence is or where his barbershop was spouts off.

"Most definitely, a B-i-i-i-g Salute to the homie Terrence out there at Faded's keeping em fresh, North Philly style ya'll!

"No doubt homie see you tonight!"

Skrilla leans back and puts his phone back into his pocket under the cape. Terrence gives him a slight pound on his shoulder with his fist as a Thank You for the plug on the air. The Dj continues speaking on air as the haircut resumes.

"Well, there you have it folks! Skrilla Kay! Haircut, check! Dope rhymes, check! Dope chain, check! Tonight doors open at 9:00! If you ain't there you're nowhere! Let's jump into that new Skrilla Kay joint right now!"

Chain Reaction begins the blaring out the speakers and Lil E. fly's out of his chair dancing around the barbershop. Skrilla reaches behind him for the remote and lowers the radio to stop his partner from making a fool out of himself. Lil E dances across the floor to shake Skrilla's hand like he hadn't noticed the radio had been lowered, dancing as if it was still blaring in his head only. He leans in hyping, quickly realizing that handshake was going to get in the way of the haircut and diverts to tapping Skrilla on the knee.

"Wooooooo ooooh woooooh. You have arrived Skrillz!!!"

Unable to fully share in the excitement Skrilla looks at Lil E in disbelief. He began to feel the roller-coaster going up. It was the feeling of knowing that he was completely not in control of his situation, coupled with the fact that he's put all control in the hands of his dancing homie.

"Yeah, You heard that right?!" he says catching E.'s attention, referring to two words only, Chain and Check. At this point the groove was interrupted and the dancing stopped. E's face straightened up as he dialed into Skrilla's eyes while mouthing "I gotchu my G!".

Terrence being no stranger to the street could sense in the air that something wasn't right.

"You see what I'm talkin bout?! I hope all this shit ain't go'n in one ear and out the other. I wanna see you win Skrillz. I don't want nothing from you. I'd just rather know winners than losers ya heard? Ya'll just gotta work wit each other that's all! Skrilla's the head of y'all operation. When you in a fight what part of the body do you guard?

Lil E. Has a small glimpse of shame as he answers. "The head.....right."

Skrilla looks at Lil E. with a smirk that states he is well aware of his bullshit and is starting to understand the barber more and more as each second goes by.

# Chapter Six

Sandwiched in by the all black neighborhoods of West Lehigh ave and the all white neighbor-hoods of East Lehigh lies the heart of little Puerto Rico. Graffiti and two story high murals of North Philly's fallen Latin hustling heroes lace the walls of the Badland's streets. This is also the heart of the North Philadelphian drug trade and literally the drug capital of the world. Now, the once Fortune 500 worthy street corners have been reduced to hundreds of mom and pop shops scattered about in a fight for their lives with a lingering air of the money raked in off these very same streets years ago.

On the corner of Mascher and Cambria, the line between commercial and residential had clearly been blurred. Thirty houses on the block, thirteen were missing, eleven abandoned, and six occupied, yet there was always at least fifteen people outside on the sidewalk daily. Ghetto's all over the world share a great deal of things in common, yet there was simply no place on Earth equivalent to North Philly. In fact, just when you begin to think they're all the same you will find what's posted up on this corner, standing as proud as the stop sign, as if he was supposed to be there. A twenty-two year old Puerto Rican covered in tattoos from the neck down, with a huge beard sticking off of his chin, a v-neck white t-shirt, pink pajama pants sitting on a pair of worn down fuzzy teddy bear slippers, and of course a twenty-five caliber pistol tied around his thigh. This was Manny.

Fresh off of a six month stint for a probation violation, Manny was back on the block to reclaim what he considered to be his, the four corners of Mascher and Cambria. Unfortunately for him, he was a recipient of a gift as well as a curse. He was in a neighborhood that supported him in thinking it was his right to hustle, the gift. On the other hand, there were a whole lot of others who shared that very same sentiment, the curse. He had been raised by the hustlers on the block from the age of nine, running back and fourth to the store for them and occasionally carrying the drugs off of the block during minor police raids. When it came to the streets, he had seen it all. Now that he was of age, he found himself attempting to duplicate his childhood for the young children on the street that were also trusted into the street life, but the damaged economy prevented his picture from developing in the same way. It was the memories of his neighborhood's glorious past that kept him in constant competition with himself, along with the fading mural of his uncle who had achieved an immortal status in streets of North Philly.

In the midst of his recent vacation two different crews had formed on his street, one at the top of the block and one in the middle. Manny and his young band of misfits controlled the bottom end of the street, which was actually a better location because being at the bottom of a one-way left the cops only one direction to pull up on rather than two. He was awarded the block mostly by way of nepotism and inheritance, but he could have quite possibly earned it on his own merit if given the opportunity. Although things weren't always consistent for him, he would remain consistent, posting on the block with or without product. He became a staple of his neighborhood and community.

While Manny frustrates himself by staring at the cars pulling up at the end of the block and customers walking directly towards his competition, his attention is diverted by a loud voice approaching the corner.

"Y'all know what it is. I got it by the tons! Musica, aqua, and bonita bun buns! Check it out today fellas?"

"Nah Poppy, I can't fuck wit you today. I'm fucked up. Shit is real!" Manny says honestly, declining the offer to check out the products.

"Yeah, real rough out here." The roaming entrepreneur responds while laughing.

Manny's youngest crew member age nine going on nineteen pulls up on his bmx bike and proudly blurts out at the hustler. "Hold on whatchu got Pa?"

Not in the mood for his worker's inquiry, Manny sucks his teeth and jumps in.

"Watchu got? Lil muhfucka whatchu got?! You ain't got no bread!"

A slight hint of embarrassment covers the face of the youngster as the man laughs and continues stepping off of the corner turning the block.

"Aight y'all be good."

"Aight Fam." Manny replies while looking up the block.

Just under a minute later a customer walks toward Manny and subtly gestures his hands signaling for one bag of their product. Manny signals his worker across the street. "Yeerrrrrooh!" The worker then signals into the alley where another worker is. "Ooo oool!" The worker in the alley then signals a next worker in the back of an abandoned building that connects to the alley. "Kahhk Kaaah!" This was an overly extravagant way of doing things over one dime bag of weed, but Manny would insist his corner operate in this fashion due to the way he was trained. It was a hard thing for him to admit that he was trained in an era where it was actually worth all of the trouble.

Eventually the bag ends up in the hands of Manny's youngest worker who then makes the transaction. Just before walking off the customer shakes the money into Manny's hand. Manny is now visibly frustrated with his current financial situation. Looking at the other crews on the block outselling his ten to one, he begins to boil over.

"Yo this is bullshit! The whole fuck'n street get'n paid except us! These niggaz got Blueberry! They got Sour Apple! What the fuck we got? How much we got left till re-up?"

"We only got one more! But I hope it's something different coming cause this shit looks like dog shit!"

"Shit. It might be, cause it smell like it too!" another worker interjects.

"Chill! I added it all up. After we dump the rest of this shit and my sister Jessica lets me the rest, then we got enough for that good shit! Some Mango, Strawberry and Kiwi Kush, Niggaz! Den the block gone be ours again!" Affirms Manny.

Manny and the crew begin hearing a loud beeping sound reminiscent of an alarm on and old cheap digital watch. His workers all simultaneously look to their legs at the ankle cuffs they are wearing like jewelry.

"I just came home, it ain't me! That's one of y'all shits!"

"I know it ain't me! I ain't got one!" the youngest employee chimes in from the comfort of his bike seat.

"Shit, you should have one by next week right?" Manny replies with a bit of jealousy.

Breaking all the confusion, one of Manny's workers shouts out in a panic. "Damn that's me. I'm out I'll be back after six!"

While drug traffic continues on the block without involving Manny's crew, Manny tries to secure the rest of the necessary funds for his re up. After several rings Jessica answers from the jewelry store.

"Come on Manuel I told you I got you but I haven't got paid yet."

"Damn Jessy what the fuck! Damn I need you this time, this shit is crazy out here. This shit get'n outta control. You know this ain't like me. I can't take this shit. This can't go down like this! You know how I roll! I don't wanna go back. What's up?...Huh?...Oh yeah, aight! Say no more Jessita!"

An extremely upset Manny hangs up the phone just as another customer approaches the corner and signals for two bags.

"We only got one more Fam!" Explains Manny.

"Nah we got more." The young hustler says from his bike.

"What the fuck?!!? You said we only had one more!"

"Yeah, one more bundle. Yeeerrroh!!"

Manny stands on the corner pissed off, breathing heavily from his nose while subtly contemplating his existence.

"Can't believe this Shit!"

# Chapter Seven

Nestled on the edge of Nicetown across from the train station, lies the cable company and more importantly Skrilla's place of employment. This was a commitment he'd made to himself after a string of botched attempts at getting paid he and Lil E had endured. His absence in the office was vaguely felt throughout the building leaving his fate in the hands of a mood swinging coworker. This was a situation that Skrilla was much smarter than, but it was one of the days where you have to put it all on the line, and he cautiously attempted to do so.

Kim sits at the front counter with her phone neatly position for her eyes only, exercising her index finger surfing through pictures online. She puts her mood thru a silent blender while happily looking pictures she had posted, to angrily looking at posts of six packs in the gym, only to find something funny and laugh seconds later. She was what most people would consider to be a fairly insecure person due to her issues with her weight, yet would have no trouble being hit on daily, just never by the types of men that she was attracted to. An emotional roller coaster is what she would find herself traveling on most days and couldn't seem to find the control that she truly wanted over her life. This would occasionally be taken out on anyone around her. Despite her personality flaws, she was actually an extremely responsible young woman and was definitely the most responsible employee of the cable company that she was overqualified for. This is what made her employment and life so troubling to her, constantly seeing people less qualified and far less responsible enjoying life and relationships in a way that she only dreamt about.

While progressing through another annoyingly normal day of work, two female customers of the ratchet persuasion enter the cable company's doors and step into the line at the cable company. One is loudly speaking into her phone somewhere between yelling and speaking obnoxiously while the other approaches the reception desk.

"Why you can't grab my other kids somethin' when you at the store? You don't make no sense. What I'm pose to give my daughter somethin' and you not have nothin' for the boys?What? It don't matter if they not ya kids, they ya daughter's brothers, I mean dayum!" She loudly barks into her phone desperately trying to assure that everyone hears her conversation, believing they will share her opinion.

"Can I help you?" Kim says to the woman at the counter while silently disgusted at her friends conversation. The customer hands Kim a wrinkled bill from her purse and stares at her.

"Would you like to pay this bill Mam? Oh wait a minute, It seems this bill is from a few months ago."

"No, I didn't come here to pay no bills. I need one of my boxes fixed." She says while laughing confidently.

"I did all the phone stuff, somebody gotta come out and give me a new box."

Kim's frustration level begins to climb while looking at the two young women. She thought to herself, "What am I a mind reader? How you gonna hand me an old bill as if I'm supposed to know you need your box replaced?". She let out a breath and calmly responded while looking into her computer screen,

"Um...ok...Let me see...We can have someone come out tomorrow morning if that's alright with you."

"Uhn-ahn! Not in the morning cause we gone be at the Stadium tonight and I'ma be too damn tired in the morning! Come on now, that Career Criminals show is gonna be lit tonight!"

Kim very quietly sucks her teeth at the young lady's comment while masking it as something on her computer screen that was upsetting her as she responds.

"How's Monday at two?"

"So she ain't gonna have no TV all day Sunday? Uh Ahnn, y'all gotta adjust her bill for that. Ain't nobody payin' for no tv that they ain't got!" The young woman on the phone says loudly injecting herself into the conversation, also while showing no regard to the person whose ear she was yelling in.

Kim subtly returns fire at the two young women. "Sure Mam, you just contact us when you're ready to

pay your balance and that will be adjusted for you."
She says putting an emphasis on the word pay.

The two customer head for the door feeling complete and accomplished. Just before crossing the threshold to the pavement outside of the cable company, the loudmouth young woman that Kim was happy to see go can be heard pausing from driving her daughter's father absolutely mad saying to her friend, "...And girl you know Skrilla Kay gonna be there...wit his sexy self!"

This was enough to push Kim's mood over her limit as she looks up at the clock which now reads 10:30 am. Letting her frustration get the best of her and taking the opportunity to not be available to help Skrilla during her lunch break, Kim yells back toward the office. "Can I take an early lunch today Ronnie?"

"Hell nah! Y'all think I'm in here for play. Your lunch time is your lunch time!"

Feeling completely under appreciated by both Skrilla and Ronnie, Kim picks up her phone to return to her normal position of finger surfing through her social media.

"...And I don't want you flick'n through that phone while at the desk either! Only phone I want you on belongs to this cable company!"

Ronnie's barking is quickly interrupted by a slamming sound from one of his newest employees that was now doing Skrilla's job dropping a brand new cable box onto the floor.

# Chapter Eight

While on the northern side of North Philadelphia the sound of a brand new cable box hitting the floor rings throughout the cable company's interior, the sound of a thirteen year old hand jumping up and slapping a stop sign resonates off of the corner outside of the barbershop where Skrilla and Lil E are now exiting.

"Aight y'all be good. Remember what I told y'all!" Terrence reiterates while shaking the hands of the two before they hit the now scorching pavement outside of the shop. He gives Skrilla a firm shake and reminds him to "Tear it down tonight!", then gives E a shake along with a quick pat on the shoulder signifying that he doesn't hate him, he is just interested in seeing him do better by his friend.

"Yeah no doubt T! Good look'n on the cut! Got a nigga fresh!"

"Aight T..." Lil E calmly mutters feeling like pat on the back was a handout that he didn't want or need.

"You make sure you tear it the fuck up tonight Skrillz!"

"All the way T! I'ma get at you fam. Appreciate you!"

"Aight now scram, ya'll got me air conditioning the whole city right now!" He says while chuckling and dusting off the sea for his next customer.

The shop door closes and the two head off down the street. Skrilla can't help but wonder to himself where exactly the two are headed, knowing that he should be headed towards the jewelry store and that time was against him. Before getting the opportunity to ask the question that was that was the only significant conversation the two should be having at his time "Where's ya man?", his thought was briefly interrupted by a fully confident E spouting off.

"...Ol hate'n ass Terrence! Them old niggaz always think they try'n to school a nigga. Wit that ol hate'n ass talk. Nigga talk'n bout fuck'n groupies ain't a job. Nigga? That nigga wish he was get'n some groupie ass!

"Nah, Terrence ain't no hater. He been do'n his thing! Why you think some people come in there call'n that nigga Butta? Trust me he's known! You know that, how you think he got the shop?"

"What?! That wrinkled ass barbershop! That ain't bout shit. Ol two and a half chairs in that muhfucka! That's what niggaz do when they get old and weak. They say fuck it let me get a barbershop or hair salon round the way. That nigga can't fool me wit that shit!" Lil E says mostly out of resentment, knowing that Terrence had the ability to see through him like a clean glass window, trying to give the perception that it was really the other way around to restore his dignity.

"So watchu say'n he pose to turn into Pablo Escobar out here or he ain't shit?! That nigga ain't fall off. Them niggaz he use to roll wit fell off. Shit they all dead!"

"That niggaz crew died from old age nigga!" E fires back with his final jab.

"Yeah aight. So what's good, where we go'n? Yo fucks up wit ya man? Fuck all the bullshit!"

"Chill homie, I just hollered at him when we was at the shop! Everything is cool. He said he's on the way over here, he just gotta make a stop. But he's come'n. I told him what it was. Shit let's just shoot over my crib for a minute. He said he gone call when he over here, plus it's getting hot enough to light a blunt on the sidewalk!"

"Damn you just fuck'n me all up! I wanna go get that shit out the way! Man!" Skrilla says while sighing, realizing that his day was spiraling out of control and that he had know choice but to roll with E to keep track of what's going on.

"Shit just hit them niggaz up. They ain't go'n nowhere. Tell em to have ya jawn all cleaned up and you'll be over there early afternoon that's all."

"Yo you know this is some bullshit!"

Skrilla pulls out his phone which is full of contacts and vigorously looks for the store's number, but can't manage to find it.

"Damn I swore I had it in here. Shit!"

"What, to the store? Man they got that shit all over the place that 215 555-gold shit."

"Oh yeah. Damn I'm buggin!"

"Yeah, you slip'n my G."

Skrilla dials the jewelry store only to find out the number is not in service. He hangs up the phone and let's out a long gust of air until his lungs are almost empty. In complete disbelief, he realizes his day is getting more and more complicated by the second and continues walking toward E's house anticipating the arrival of E's homie and more importantly his money.

"This shit ain't even in service. What the fuck!"

"Chill out my G, you know they over there. Relax!"

As the two pass the corner of Somerset St a car passes by and the driver yells out of the window at Skrilla, "Skrilla! What up!"

"Yo yo!" Skrilla replies trying to hide the fact that he is quickly becoming drained by the way is day is unfolding. After cutting the corner onto Lehigh Avenue and nearing the outside of E's house, Skrilla continues.

"That's easy for you to say, but I'm the one that's gotta deliver. That's the type of shit Terrence was talk'n bout."

"Man that nigga talk'n bout niggaz who ain't do'n shit. All the work I put in?! Shiiit...."

"Huh? Now I'm lost. What work you put in?!"

"What nigga?! I'm your street cred!"

The comment immediately stops Skrilla in his tracks.

"My what?! Get the fuck outta here. I'm good out here! And you say'n that's because of you? You gotta be kidding me! Remember when I punched Gary in the face for you and you didn't even jump in? You're my street cred?"

"Man, we was like nine years old!"

"And he was thirteen! Anyway..."

"Look homie, I put in work out here. I'm do'n this shit for us! The team!" E says trying reassert himself and restore his pride once again.

"Yeah aight Playboy! You're my street cred." Skrilla replies laughing it off, though E seriously believed what he was saying.

Arriving outside of the house E and Skrilla's frivolous conversation continues while they pause briefly by the steps. An old women watches the two from a vantage point in a bedroom window next door to E's house. Skrilla takes a seat on the front steps while E stands on the sidewalk leaning on the rail reaching into his pocket for another jar of weed. He twists off the cap to take a whiff before getting ready roll up another spliff.

"Whew! This thing smells like shit! I gotta stop fuck'n wit these cats!"

"I thought it smelled funny. Where did you get that bullshit anyway?"

"From the Rican cats on Cambria... I heard they had fire around there. This shit smells like it was burnt already."

Skrilla shakes his head and looks E and returns to the previous topic.

"My street cred huh? Blow'n on dirt out here."

Quickly changing the conversation E stuffs the jar back into his pocket and excitedly tells Skrilla, "Yo I didn't tell you bout the jawn from last night. That ass was right! I had that thing do'n cartwheels in here dog. For real!"

Just as the words leave his mouth he makes eye contact with an old woman in the window next door watching and listening to them. Skrilla chuckles at his comment and a slightly embarrassed E taps his arm and gestures for him to come into the house.

"Come on let's go in the crib man. All eyes on me like I'm Tupac ya dig."

"Yeah aight." Skrilla replies getting up and following him into the house.

# Chapter Nine

Walking into nineteen seventy-nine E's grandmother remains positioned exactly where she was when he had left. E attempts to scoot past her television and slide downstairs without disturbing her soap opera watching when he is interrupted in mid stride by Skrilla greeting his grandmother.

"Hello Ms. Robin, How's everything going today?"

Being used to E constantly sliding company down the stairs she recognizes the sound of Skrilla's voice and her face lights up with a bright smile as she looks away from the television.

"Is that that handsome Khalil?" She says putting he glasses on that we're hanging on a chain around her neck.

"Well, of course it is! How you do'n baby? And how's that pretty young girlfriend of yours doin? Tasha...right?"

"Yes, Mam I'm fine, everybody's doing well."

"That's good, I'm so glad for you. So, you ready for your big concert tonight? I know you've got to be excited." She says completely shocking the both of them, proving she hasn't lost a step.

"Yes, Mam! I'm ready. Hopefully it will lead to bigger things for all of us."

"Oh it will! It's a Chain Reaction." She says smiling, enjoying the fact that she is now doubling down on shocking the two of them. "There's some hash on the stove if you're hungry, ok now..."

"No Thank you Ms. Robin, I ate this morning but thank you." Skrilla politely tells her while slowly walking toward E and the basement door.

"Grandma, we've got some business to attend to down here" says E with a slight degree of jealousy at how nicely his friend is being treated.

"Mmmmhhmmm..." She replies to E immediately jumping back into her normal tone. E trudges down the stairs with Skrilla quietly following behind him. After descending down into E's basement paradise Skrilla plops down into his cracked leather recliner and looks toward E shaking head with half of a smile.

"Still bring'n jawns all through Grandma's huh?"

"Shit, this my crib! All the electric, gas, and water, that's me dog." Replies E with an ignorant and arrogant sense of confidence, completely oblivious to the fact that he is talking to someone who knows almost everything about him. While stewing in his oblivion E reaches for his laptop and flips it open. The screen is plastered with the biggest booties in bikinis that he could find on the net. He leans back and quickly opens his browser to pull up the latest rap battle. Skrilla reluctantly begins getting comfortable and ready's himself to watch the battle, knowing that it was about to swallow at least thirty minutes of his much needed time.

"This is draw'n! What's good?" Skrilla says referring to the fact that he has a busy day lined up and E is apparently in another world.

"Come on, do we really have to go thru this again? I got you! He's on his way. What are we supposed to do, stare at the wall until he gets here?"

Skrilla lets out a gasp of air and E begins skimming thru his phone trying to recall the name of his date from last night.

"What was her name? Damn. Maria, ok! Shit she look like a Maria." He says smiling, feeling like the Hugh Hefner of North Philadelphia. He turns up the volume on his laptop, but not before sparking the unfinished blunt he was smoking previously. Just as the battle begins the apartment begins to fill with smoke as E blows out a cloud like a train passing through the basement. He leans over and passes the blunt to Skrilla who declines while disappointingly shaking his head. The sound begins to blare from a set of speakers positioned in different spots all over the room.

"Round 1 your go!"

"Aight, look...I gotta style you can believe in/ You gotta style they rake leaves in!"

The two begin chuckling as E spouts out "GOD!..."

# Chapter Ten

"**D**ammit!!" One of Philadelphia's finest says as if he was finishing E's statement, spilling a bit of hot coffee on his hand as he and his partner hit one of the city's potholes on the corner of Darien Street before turning onto Lehigh Avenue.

"You alright over there Rook?" The driver says with a sense of authority.

"Why do you keep calling me rookie? I know it's my first week but you've only been a cop for a month!"

"When you're patrolling in the Badlands Rook, everyday out here counts!"

The two are quickly interrupted at the stop sign by the sight of Manny and six of his employees from the block slowly pedaling an array of bmx bikes up Lehigh Avenue towards Germantown. The two officers both paused in awe at the spectacle they were witnessing. Manny had now ventured off of the block in his pink pajama pants, on a purple girls bike with sparkles on the frame, slowly pedaling up the street with his face screwed up like gangster followed by his band of misfits. His crew quite efficiently added to the show while on a variety of bikes, including one with no seat, brakes, or anything that would be considered normal, all pedaling with purpose in their eyes as if carrying out a military assignment. The officers pause at yet another North Philly anomaly as the cluster passes directly in front of their car ignoring their presence and authority.

"See what I mean Rook?"

Back at the jewelry store Mark and Eli are deep in a casual conversation speaking in Russian while sitting down behind the counter in folding chairs. Jessica is also having an extremely frivolous conversation on her cell phone in Spanish while on the customer's side of the display case, wiping it down with a spray bottle and cloth, ignoring her boss's conversation while they are equally ignoring hers. The two conversations are even in volume and frivolousness as well. The Russians are drinking coffee like water and smoking cigarettes like oxygen. Eli reaches for a bottle of vodka neatly positioned under the counter getting ready to pour a shot into his coffee.

"Hey, let me call you back." Jessica says in Spanish after noticing a customer at the door through the glass. She hangs up the phone and quickly moves to the employee side of the display case. Mark immediately buzzes the door after Jessica makes her way around the counter. The buzzer sounds as the door opens and all conversation comes to an immediate halt and is changed to a simultaneous "Hello."

The customer enters the store. He is a young man a year or two younger than Jessica and does not appear to be able to afford anything in the store.

"Yes, can I help you with something?" Jessica says with her glowing smile. Mark quickly jumps out of his chair and interrupts.

"Let me handle this one Jessica."

Mark moves over to directly in front of the main display case where Jessica stands.

"What's up my man? Look'n to get iced out! What can I get for you my man? You talk to me!"

"Umm...I was just..."

"Look here my man. Don't worry, anything in here you see, you can have. Don't worry about the price tag, we can work that out for you my man!"

The young man looks into the display in awe staring directly onto a jewelry tray of the stores best and brightest, with prices from $2400 to $3800.

"Nah I think I'm cool, I just..."

"Check it out my man! I can see you are a smart and savvy business man like myself. This, I only show to other businessmen like ourselves!" Mark says while looking directly into the mind of the youngster. Jessica routinely pass's Mark a tray of very inexpensive imitation jewelry that looked ridiculously cheap with plastic diamonds inside of what barely resembled gold.

"As you can see my friend, all of these look exactly the same."

The customer points at one of the rings after being sucked into Mark's magical advances.

"How much for this one?" He says pointing to the largest and blatantly the gaudiest of them all."

"This one my man? For you? Give me a hundred and it's yours! This is an easy $150 I sell this for!"

"Uh, I ain't got it right now. I gotta come back another time."

"Aww man buddy! I really want for you to have this ring Buddy, but if someone comes I gotta let it go Buddy."

He then takes a step back getting ready to leave just as a determined Mark attempts to reel him back in.

"How much we got? What we work'n wit? Talk to me partner come on!"

The customer pulls out a ten dollar bill and quietly mumbles "All I got is this ten dollars."

Mark then leans in and puts his hands on the money and the boy let's go.

"That's perfect because all we need is ten percent my friend! This ring is now yours Buddy!"

Jessica again in a very routine fashion hands Mark a brown jewelry envelope and Mark puts the ring in it and pulls the tag off of the envelope and gives it to the customer. Mark extends his hand to shake the customer's hand.

"Don't worry Buddy! It will be right here when you want to pick it up!"

The customer backs up as the door buzzes and walks out of the door in a complete stupor. Before the door has a chance to close it swings back open and a very stressed looking Mr. Jung walks into the establishment. Mark neatly slides the money into his pocket not wanting his landlord to see the register opening. He didn't want to give him the slightest whiff of money in the air while is face quickly transformed into is signature plastic smile. Jessica sits down and Eli steps up behind the display case next to Mark allowing him the opportunity to work his magic the way they've unfortunately become accustomed to doing on a monthly basis.

"What's up my friend Mr. Jung? How are you doing today?" Mark says with an irremovable smile similar to that of a wax figure.

"Yes, I'm just here for rent." Mr. Jung says looking directly into Mark's smile, subconsciously knowing that he was not about to be handed the cash that he'd come for.

"Yes, of course, and we will have that for you right away! But you see it's actually on the way here. I would give it to you now but we only have small money in register for giving change. You understand?"

"No, no, no! I'm here for rent. You know I'm coming today. Today is rent day!"

"We will have the rent for you today. What he says is true, we are actually expecting it now at any minute." Eli interjects.

"No, no, no!! Today is rent day. I don't have time for this now! You know today is rent day! This is not acceptable!"

"Mr. Jung, your money is on the way shortly. You're the man Mr. Jung! We know we've got to pay the man! You will have your money today my friend, that's for sure."

Eli is looks towards the door, spotting a customer and buzzes the door.

"You see here Mr. Jung we have very very serious clientele here, rappers and the likes."

Just as Mark speaks to the level of clientele the store has, the door is buzzed and Manny bursts in.

Manny is the exact opposite of the clientele Mark was trying to describe, with his pajama pants dragging on the floor under the backs of his fuzzy slippers, not to mention the cast of characters he had waiting for him outside of the store visibly thru the window.

He burst into the store and looks at Mr Jung and his sister. Disguising his need for the money with the want to avenge his little sister, Manny speaks loudly and boldly as if he were standing on the corner of his beloved block.

"What's up Chino?" He says quickly acknowledging Mr. Jung. "I got you Jessita! Don't even worry!"

Manny looks at the two Russians and randomly picks Eli to address.

"You! What's up nigga?! I'm hear'n my sister works and can't get paid! What's up with that shit nigga?!"

"Oh no, of course she will be paid my friend." Mark replies, jumping into to the now fully embarrassing and uncomfortable position they were thrusted into. Manny couldn't have chosen a worse time to come to the store if he tried to.

"Nah fam! This ain't wit you! I'm talk'n to this nigga!" Manny says directing his attention back to Eli.

"Well nigga?! Tell me something nigga! You thought you was gonna just ride all over my lil sister nigga?!"

"We can assure you Jessica will be payed today my good friend!" Mark calmly states to him.

"I told you Bro, this between me and this nigga!"

Jessica is utterly embarrassed and flies out of her seat to address her brother and attempt to remove him from the store.

"Manny, chill! What the fuck! I told you later on! This is my job! You can't just do that!"

Mr Jung's frustration meter quickly begins to rise as he decides to back out of the commotion and exit the store.

"Look guys the rent today! No excuses!"

"What?! This nigga owe you too Chino!? Ay Jessy I'm telling you, this nigga think he slick! I'ma be back! For real I ain't even play'n wit you nigga!"

Mr. Jung looks at the two as he proceeds towards the door.

"I'll be back today for the rent today guys."

"Yeah Chino! I'll be back today too! Nigga! You could bet on that. You better have that bread right next time I come here nigga!"

Manny and Mr. Jung exit the store with Manny bursting through the door just as hard as he came in and Mr. Jung follows directly after. Manny's crew is sitting on their bikes patiently waiting for him to lead the group of cronies back to their block. Manny grabs the handle bar of his bike and flings the bike up. "Yo we out!" He blurts, feeling slightly accomplished while the group follows suit and begins pedaling away down Germantown Ave. Mr Jung unconsciously shakes his head attempting to shake off his frustration as well as the sight of Manny and his crew from his head. He walks about two parking spaces down from the store to the passenger side of a white minivan and opens the door. Just as he opens the door his wife, Mrs. Jung comes with a cardboard box full of things, and puts it on the backseat of the minivan. Mr. Jung heads to the driver seat and starts the van while she grabs another box and places it on the seat. She hops into the passenger seat and angrily looks over at Mr Jung.

"They pay?!"

"Today they pay! Calm down. They will pay!"

"It now 1:00 and still no pay!"

Mrs. Jung begins to heavily curse out her husband in Chinese as she slams the van door, before Mr. Jung slowly pulls out of the parking spot into the slow moving traffic on Germantown Avenue. The air condition starts to blow warm air on top of the scorching summer heat and Mr. Jung cuts it off while letting out a sigh and rolling the windows down as his wife begins to curse louder as things now begin to heat up figuratively as well as literally.

# Chapter Eleven

While several blocks away on Germantown Avenue the Jung's van attempts to slowly crawl thru traffic, the minivan of the Philadelphia Parking Authority is slowly cruising down E's block searching for a vehicle on the city's boot list. Skrilla walks out and posts on the steps outside of the house, leaning in the door frame nonchalantly looking at the van coming down the street towards them.

"Damn man this shit is take'n all dizzay. Shit!"

"Nah every things cool he should be coming around any second. Oh shit!!" Lil E yells out as if he'd just seen a grenade go off, spotting the parking authority's van and running back into the house.

"Oh shit get in the wheel!"

"Its open?" Skrilla replies calmly complying without realizing the severity of the situation.

"You know my shit don't lock! Get in!!"

Skrilla shakes his head and gets in on the passenger side of the car. Before he has the chance to close the door Lil E. comes flying out of the house with keys in his hand and runs to the driver side door. He jumps in the car and tries to start the car. He again is in between hope and prayer trying to use a combination of both to pull off yet another trick.

"Damn what the fuck no gas! Come on dog, you serious?" Skrilla utters, again in disbelief at the situations his friend ends up in.

"Chill I got this...she gone start! Come on baby!"

The Parking Authority, who spent their days circling like sharks in open water searching for prey was the enemy of everyone in the city of Philadelphia and was now nearing E's boot worthy vehicle. Again trying vigorously to start the car, it's beginning to seem like today is the day his beloved car will end up in the jaws of the shark, as the driver realizes the vehicle has racked up $420 in tickets.

"Shit! Come on baby, come on girl!

"You really, really can't be fuck'n serious. This is the bullshit!"

The van's driver hops out of the van weighing in at about a solid three hundred and fifty pounds and smelling like the cutting board of a sandwich shop. He slides open the van door and with one hand grabs a heavy yellow boot out of the back of the van and waddles over to the back of E's car exuding a combination of extreme fatness and extreme strength. The slamming sound of the boot next to E's back wheel becomes the sound of a cruel reality. The two remain speechless in the cockpit of the car as the officer heads back to his van for his bag of tools. Lil E stares at the steering wheel in a twisted mixture of silently praying and begging. The driver approaches the vehicle returning with the tools to seal E's fate and slams the bag of heavy metal tools on the ground. E stares at the steering wheel as if looking into another dimension and whispers. "Come on baby!"

Without any thought or cognition the car's engine turns over, also turning over the cloud of gloom beginning to set in over their circumstances. In an effortless motion the car was thrown into drive and the duo peels out of the parking spot leaving the unfazed parking officer left standing and staring at the rear of the Caprice peeling off down the street. Business as usual consumes his face while he begins picking up the boot and undoing what he had just done in the same unenthusiastic fashion that he started.

Pulling directly into the gas station on the corner of 5th and Lehigh Avenue, another reality sets in for Skrilla who is finally able to gather his words and speak again.

"Damn you my ride tonight! No gas! Bout to get booted?! God damn!"

"Chill big homie! I got you!" E says pulling a wrinkled five dollar bill from his pocket to put another drop of hope into the tank of his car. He approaches the window of the gas station and strategically says, "Put that on three!". A loud crackling speaker can be heard throughout the gas station lot saying, "Yes sir five on three!" E refuses to allow it to break his stride or his confidence as he approaches the pump and begins pumping.

"Five on three huh? What does this muthafucka run on magic or something? Let me know! Shit if that's the case can you pull this guy and my bread out of a top hat please...Shit!

After the pump quickly begins to click E hangs it up and jumps back into the car brushing off Skrilla's attacks as well as the gas light that was barely off and could quite possibly be coming back on in the extremely near future. Skrilla sinks down into the seat and throws his glasses on trying to preserve the image he'd created in the streets as the dynamic duo approach the busy intersection of Germantown Avenue. A small glimmer of hope fills the car when E's phone begins ringing but is quickly defused when he looks at it and doesn't answer. Skrilla shrugs and decides to take in the view of the sweaty North Philadelphians passing by.

"Un-fucking-believable!" He mumbles under his breath.

"So where we go'n? Tell me we're about to go get wit ya man, that's all I'm try'n to hear right now!" Skrilla says after realizing the two were now driving away from E's house and more importantly driving away from his money. The day was now dancing on the border line between early and late. For normal working people it could no longer be considered early by any stretch of the imagination, but on the Badland streets the day was still in its infancy.

"Yo Skrillz I'm not bullshit'n you. For real my nigga! He's coming over here. Shit I got my phone wit me as soon as he calls I'm on his top!"

"Man hit the bul up and tell him I need that! I ain't got time for this shit today!"

Reaching into his pocket he slowly pulls out his phone knowing this wasn't a conversation that he wanted to have in front of his homie, although he remained with a blinding confidence that his business associate was on his way into the neighborhood and was going to make good on their agreement. He scrolls through the phone while approaching the light and tries to divert his attention once again.

"I'm say'n...I just talked to him a lil minute ago and he told me he was on the way over this way. I ain't try'n to keep hit'n him up. He know I'm on his top already!"

"Man! On his top huh? I'm on ya top! On somebody's top must mean not getting paid because everybody seems to be on everybody's top, but nobody's getting paid!"

"Yea...aight...you know I got you, besides you gotta get that check right?"

"Shit! You right, it's damn near 1:30! Turn up here on Broad!"

E was once again maintaining his position as both gift and curse for Skrilla. He was certainly the cause of ninety-nine percent of the stress he was carrying for the day, but somehow managed to circumvent that fact by reminding him of what was necessary at the most opportune times for the both of them. Besides the years of history between them, it was this that had become a huge ingredient to the glue that bound them together.

"Woah!!!!"

"What the fuck!!!" They shout simultaneously as E slams his foot down on the break pedal.

"You see that? This guy is crazy!" E says loudly watching Mr. Jung nonchalantly roll through the light almost causing them to slam into his driver side door. With beads of sweat dripping down his face Mr.Jung looks over at the two without a care in the world for the near drastic collision he'd almost caused.

Inside of the Jung's van had now become a personal hell for Mr. Jung. Not only were the two sweating profusely, but they were also in the middle of a monthly scenario that seemed to worsen every month. The tension was thick enough to be cut with a chainsaw. While his wife continued relentlessly with her rant of owning name brand products and moving their growing family into a house in the near future, Mr. Jung's head was beginning to throb. He too wanted the best for is family but was becoming consumed by his failed attempts at doing providing it. He was in a constant state of trying to restore the balance in his relationship that was becoming heavily dominated by his mother in law, rendering him outnumbered and out-strategized as well.

"I told you I will handle the store! The rent is due today! Today we will get the rent! I'm taking care of the store! No more!" He yells out interrupting her rant in the manliest tone he could muster. She looks over to him and quiets down, impressed to a small degree she sucks her teeth agreeing he's had enough for now. For a brief moment things in the car began to settle when one of the city's large busses merged lanes directly in front of the car. Mr. Jung looked up at the back of the bus and let out a gasp of air knowing exactly what's to come. His short lived moment of sanity had come to an extreme hauls as Mrs. Jung looked up at a large advertisement of a smiling Mark and Eli under bright yellow letters that read "We buy gold!". Immediately after her eyes locked on to the sign her voice began revving up like a motorcycle engine, again with profanity laced Chinese dialogue

while the two were now sweating in traffic stuck behind the image of their tenants, holding a heap of cash
and gold in their hands, smiling at them while purport-
edly laughing at their misery.

Pulling up on the corner of Germantown and
Wayne in front of a local take-out pizza shop with one
set of table and chairs and a small eat in counter lining
its front window, E taps Skrilla's arm and points to the
window.

"There she go right there yo!"

Kim can be seen sitting directly in the window happily and aimlessly scrolling through her phone while
sucking down a diet soda and taking small bites of her
second slice of the oversized slices of sausage covered pizza served at the shop.

"Yeah...shit hold up. Let me run in here and grab
this change from this girl, wit her fuck'n attitude. She
didn't even call me!"

Skrilla opens the car door and steps out and in one
complete motion sits right back down in the car closing the door and lowering his head after noticing his
manager Ronnie walking out of the neighboring deli.

"Damn that nigga Ronnie almost seen me! Go in
there and grab the check for me dog."

"He just turned the corner, you cool." E calmly
states, looking into his rear view mirror.

"Damn you can't just grab the shit for me! Whats
good wit you? All this bread you got for me and I still
put some gas in this raggedy piece of shit! And you
can't even jus grab the check?"

"Chill my G, I got you." E replies chuckling and
opening his door. Lil E flings his car door open and

walks towards the store stomping some of the Philadelphia dust from his boots catching Skrilla's eyes as yet another small unbelievable gesture from his ghetto debonaire homie.

Spotting Lil E while speaking into an earpiece, Kim tells her friend "Girl I'ma call you later, my break is up. You know I'm gonna have to hear all about this but I'ma have to talk to you later." She looks Lil E up and down as he walks over to her smiling with his normal up to no good look that happened to be a magnet for women.

"What, Mr. Skrilla can't even get out the car now? Too big to deal wit little folk huh?"

"Aw come on now why you act'n like that? I want to say you too damn pretty to be act'n like that, but it's always you pretty chicks being so damn mean."

She quickly perks up after being poked in her sweet spot, knowing that E was no stranger to dealing with attractive women and had included her into the ranks of them.

"Nah it's not that it's just...."

"Look I already know what the problem is! So many niggaz come in here talk'n bout how damn cute you are hit'n on you all day, got you treat'n me the same damn way!"

Completely flustered, she looks to him blushing and batting her eyes and responds in a sweet voice from her gentle side.

"Nah, not at all. I mean yeah, but, nah, it's not like that we're cool! What's up?"

"I need that chizzeck so I can give it to Skrillz. You know we got that show tonight. It's gonna be lit up in there!"

"Yeah, I heard about it on the radio. Sounds like everybody gone be there except me."

"What, you ain't go'n?"

Kim gasps and rolls her eyes beginning to feel played by his charm and is rapidly slipping back into the other side of her personality, the side that would make it extremely difficult to get the check from her that is. Looking into her eyes, he gently takes her phone out of her hand while also touching her hand.

"Well, you are now."

He calls his phone from her cell and swings her back into his clutches.

"Oh really?"

"Really! Just holler at me aight." E says while locked into ear eyes courting her.

Kim softly replies in an extremely seductive tone reaching into her purse for the check.

"I sure will."

E. takes the check and puts it in his pocket and back pedals towards the door.

"Tell Skrilla I said hi!" She tells him cheerfully after being fully captivated by his presentation.

With E's mission accomplished he now has broken eye contact with Kim while pushing the door open.

"Yeah, no doubt." He says swinging the door open leaving a subtle stench in the air of him telling her whatever she wanted to hear to get the check. He steps out onto the sidewalk with her eyes locked onto him, pulling out a wash rag from his back pocket and placing it on the top of his head walking to his car. Just before opening his door he is caught quickly gazing at a pair of short shorts walking into the deli. Kim rolls her eyes and snatches her purse off of the counter top as the car pulls off into traffic down the ave. Skrilla smiles at his manager smoking a cigarette on the corner from behind the tints of the passenger window while they head off towards their next mission.

"Damn, what was that all that about?"

Lil E hands Skrilla the check and complains.

"Nah man, I had to smooth it all over. She all uptight 'n shit. But I got you, of course."

"Huh? Man what's she talk'n bout? I thought she had a lil attitude. Man, what'd she say?"

"It's cool. She was in there feel'n lonely or some shit. I told her she could come out tonight. She's cool now."

"Damn! Why you tell her that?! She ain't come'n wit us!"

E laughingly replies. "Nigga I know that! I told her ass that! She gone call me later. I'ma just hit her wit some bullshit."

"Yeah like you been hit'n me wit all fuck'n month huh?! Man drop me the fuck off on South St. and let me get my shit. And what the fuck is up wit ya man?!" Skrilla says, trying to read the reaction of E's face that is conveniently locked onto the road.

"Dog! I'm drop'n you off and go'n straight to em! Have a lil' faith in ya boy, geez"

The car makes a right turn onto Broad Street and his now positioned directly behind another bus with Mark and Eli's ad on it. E flings down his glasses that were sitting on top of his head under the wash rag without mentioning what was blatantly staring them in the face. Skrilla chooses not to mention it either as E switches lanes speeding up down Broad heading to-wards South Street to drop Skrilla off. He reaches over and turns the radio up to cut the growing tension in the car while flying down Broad St.

# Chapter Twelve

The sound of a roaring subway train can be heard rippling beneath the asphalt below the corner of Broad and Allegheny Avenue, mirroring the sound of a loose dragon flying north on subterranean Broad. The train takes off and a dainty and delicate Trina is seen ushering herself up the stairs alongside several others that had jammed themselves into the subway car that afternoon. Upon reaching the last step, she takes a short but heavy breath and begins to slowly fill with excitement while heading up the street towards the steps of her apartment building. She reaches her front step without realizing how fast she had gotten there. Passing through the doorway, she pauses and back pedals after noticing that she had skated right past her mailbox without checking it. She then heads up the broad staircase of her apartment building a few envelopes heavier then when she left in the morning. The last step was a sign of relief, not only due to the fact that it was the hottest day of the year and she was on the third floor, but because it symbolized all that encompassed what a Friday meant. She was now home. She enters her apartment and drops her purse onto the counter readying herself to call Skrilla to find out where he was and how his day was going. She consciously waited until she was home to do this, accepting that his day was jam packed and wanting to give him the freedom to handle his business without looking over his shoulder. After quickly looking over the mail she walks to her refrigerator grabbing a bottle of spring water with lemon slices in it that she had prepared the previous evening. Walking toward her bedroom to kick her shoes off she holds the bottle of water in her mouth and her cellphone in her left hand dialing Skrilla, while her right hand opens the door. Upon opening the door her eyes are immediately drawn to the sight of four large shopping bags on the floor and a fully clothed Skrilla stretched out on the bed with his feet hanging off of the bed as if he'd completely passed out.

"What the?" She says while smacking his leg to wake him up.

"Now what in the hell? Khalil...Khalil! Wake up! Wake the hell up boy! You're in here sleeping?" She says with a voice full of laughter.

"Nah, I'm up. I'm up." Skrilla mumbles as he arises from the dead, stretching and sitting up.

"Boy wake up! You know I wanna see it!"

"Damn watchu got off early? What time is it?" He says yawning, leaving the dream realm and slowly re-entering reality. He pulls his phone from his pocket with one eye squinting reads, 5:37.

"Oh shit! What the fuck!"

Jumping off of the bed as if a jolt of electricity had surged through his body, he brushes past Trina and snatches his keys off of hook heading straight for the door as if he could walk thru it. A disappointed and confused Trina follows him towards the door.

"What happened? Khalil...Don't tell me you didn't pick up your chain yet! What's going on?!"

"Nah everything is cool. I gotta run though!" He says, trying to look anywhere but in her eyes.

He makes another motion for the door but is stopped by Trina grabbing hold of his hand and not letting go, searching for the truth.

"Let me guess you still wait'n on that bullshit'n ass friend of yours huh?"

Khalil answers without speaking, shaking his head and balling the fist of his free hand, completely unable to let the words "I don't have my chain" come from his mouth.

"Damn baby! I knew he was gonna do this. So he still ain't come with your money?! Uhhg!!! That friend of yours is a lame! I told you that! Baby you know I would hold you down. I'm riding with you, but you know I don't have that kind of money right now."

Skrilla's pot is now almost boiled over. He let's go of her hand and goes to the door, again completely avoiding contact with his love's eyes.

"Nah babe you trip'n! Everything is cool. I just gotta run. I'll call you!"

Just before the door closes and he takes off darting down the stairs and she hears hill yell back from the hallway. "Babe, lock the door."

Walking with the stride of a horse down Allegheney towards the corner, Skrilla abruptly comes to the realization that at the moment he has no specific destination. He squeezes his phone out of his Jean pocket and calls E without blinking or any transmission of thought. The phone begins ringing and Skrilla tries to do everything in his power to hold back from screaming his friend while simultaneously anticipating the opportunity to just that. The phone continues to ring without being answered and Skrilla immediately redials even angrier then before. The phone begins another long series of rings before being picked up on the last possible ring.

"Yizzo where you at?"

"No, where the fuck u at? This is some real bullshit your on!" Spouts Skrilla while stopping in his tracks without an ounce of patience left in his body.

"Nah I just walked out the door. I'm on the way to your crib now."

"So what the fuck? You seen your man?"

Completely avoiding the question, knowing another direct no would not be able to be conveyed over the phone, E calmly mutters. "Hold up I'm coming to you now!"

"Man! Just come to the Chinese store." After indirectly receiving the no he was desperately hoping not to hear, he continued his stride, this time much more forceful then before.

"I'm on the way!" E replies trying sound as if he was responding to the sense of urgency as diligently as he could, yet the fact would remain that no matter how he sounded he simply couldn't deliver what he was supposed to.

Skrilla hangs up the phone without giving a response, leaving E with the notion that things were a lot stickier than he had perceived and he now fully recognized his position at the root of the mess that his friend was in.

After briskly walking a few blocks, the sign of the Chinese store can be seen about a block's distance away. Amongst many other scattered thoughts the sign slowly comes into focus. The words on the sign begin to enlarge as Skrilla nears the front of the store noticing that E's car wasn't present on the block. He quietly mouthed to himself "This muthafucka! I don't believe this shit."

Skrilla cracks his knuckles while in stride and continues on down the street towards the bright yellow sign of the Chinese take-out restaurant awaiting the arrival of is partner.

Back on the corner of Cambria and Mascher Street the situation hadn't changed much for Manny, yet the block was now much more heavily populated than it was earlier that day. The streets of North Philadelphia were now awake and fully alive, but this seemed to only confound Manny's situation even more as he tried to keep his composure and make sense of the current events he was enduring. Despite the traffic on his block, Manny and crew sat on the corner idling, waiting for a small miracle to change their circumstance for the better. He sat on the corner without the motivation to even change from the pajama pants he started his day in, taking deep breaths while trying to manage the thoughts of his current condition, mixed with the thoughts of the jail he had just left, as well as the corner and status that he remembered and was unwilling to let go of. He glances at his crew engaged in frivolous conversation that he couldn't bring himself to be a part of and then takes a hard look at the transactions being made on the opposite end of his street and involuntarily leaps off of the steps in frustration.

"This is crazy! I only was gone for three weeks and we lost the whole fuck'n corner!"

"It ain't 'cuz of that. It's this shit flavored chronic we got out here that slowed it down." The youngest and most inexperienced member of his crew blurts out learning that everything isn't meant to be said by the look on Manny's face. Losing control, Manny balls up his tattooed fists and yells out as if screaming to the cosmos "Yo!"

Stepping around the corner onto the block a customer dressed in his work uniform from a phone store steps up to Manny whose crews is in place and eagerly states "What's up dog. Let me get 16 sour apples dog."

Manny sucks his teeth and nods his head in the direction of one of the crews at the top of the block, but the customer does not move.

"Damn! I said up the fuck'n block dog!"

The customer starts walking up the block towards the other dealers and then stops and turns around.

"Well, what y'all got?"

Attempting to be useful, the youngster answers. "Its like dog shit flavored...."

"Up the block dog!" Manny jumps in completely shutting the conversation down and sending the customer on his way while trying to salvage the dignity of his end of the street.

"This shit is corny!" He says to his workers but really speaking to reality that had presented itself to them. Watching the customer reach the other end of the block he zeroes in on a dealer at the other end of the street looking towards him giggling as he makes yet another sale on the street that he'd built, but in the streets of North Philadelphia all was fair in love and hustling.

"Man these dudes got me fucked up out here! I'm bout to let somebody know what it is!"

Just as the words leave Manny's mouth Big Chollie is seen near impossibly squeezing his large truck around the corner and onto the street making his way up the narrow block. Anyone who wasn't from the city would be safe in assuming that the truck couldn't possibly fit, but for a native it was a routine turn and nothing special. The crew all stare at the truck as it passes by and stops at the other end of their block.

"Here we go again." The youngster states, again unaware that it's sometimes better to remain silent. Manny sucks his teeth as the truck stops and the driver side window rolls all the way down. Big Chollie drops a black wrinkled plastic bag full of product on the ground and pulls off. The dealer picks the bag up looking straight down the street and smiles at Manny yet again.

Manny sucks his teeth hard enough to remove a molar just as one of his workers returns to the block on his bike.

"What's up y'all? We got that that new shit yet?!"

It didn't seem possible, but Manny now looks even more pissed as his situation grows more and more desperate on the corner of his rapidly depreciating real estate.

# Chapter Thirteen

With the humid Philadelphia air becoming as thick as the tension swirling around the store, Mark is now outside looking up and down the street with coffee in hand wondering where the next dollar is coming from and more importantly where is Skrilla with his payment. Letting out a gasp of air, which seems to be the common theme of the day, he tries manage his faculties and go and face the music in the form of his partner Eli, and walks back into the store. Mark walks in and heads behind the counter Eli returns from the back of the store with the calm of a raging bull.

"Nothing yet huh?! This is nonsense we don't even have phone for our customers to call!"

"Calm down my friend. This is the nature of business, it's unpredictable, for us and our customers too. He will show. He is probably on his way as we are speaking. You've heard of speaking someone up, yes?"

"Well, Mr. Business man. I predict our landlord coming down and closing our doors for good this time!

Not to mention other problems we have!" He affirms while nodding his head towards Jessica whose phone conveniently starts ringing. She picks up her phone and looks at the screen with a brief moment of hesitation.

"Hello... No..No... not yet Manuel! I told you today. What the fuck?! Damn!"

After hanging up, she then slams her phone on her lap muttering "Crazy ass...so annoying!" Mark and Eli quietly look at each other with a telepathic conversation being transferred between the two taking place at light speed, as the mood in the store grows a little more still.

Meanwhile, inside of a graffiti ridden box that was once a dilapidated row home on the corner of 8th and Lehigh Avenue, Skrilla sits in a small window sill covered in stickers, paint markers and names scratched into the window, waiting on E to finally arrive. His mind is racing while clouded, feeling that the answer to all of his problems lied with a friend and partner that had been proving himself incapable of such a responsibility. This was a fact that everyone around him understand completely but had finally began to marinate in Skrilla's mind at the worst possible time. He felt he was in limbo in a parallel universe and that he was supposed to be preparing to shut the city down on stage in a few hours but couldn't stomach the thought of it in his current position. He sat staring into the abyss while appearing to stare thru the store's window unbeknownst to the fact that he was being stared at by an angry Mrs. Jung on the other side of the large bulletproof glass between them. He lethargically rises and begins pacing the tiny restaurant floor. A young female customer walks into the store and glances at Skrilla before looking up at the picture of all the Chinese food platters. Mrs. Jung leans on the counter and taps on the window.

"Yes, what you want?!"

"Uh...you know what, let me get a....Ah..jus give me two candy bags and a roll of toilet paper."

"$1.75!"

She pulls two wrinkled bills from her pocket and slides the money through the slot looking back at Skrilla.

"Whats her fuck'n problem?!"

Off in another, world Skrilla shruggs his shoulders while mrs. Jung begins to aggressively tap the window again.

"You need a bag? Here!"

The girl takes her things and exits the store answering her ringing phone. Reaching the pavement Skrilla can hear her on the phone."Girl, guess who I just seen?...He real as shit!"                    He sits back down and the sound of a text message coming to his phone can be heard in the store garnering the attention of he and Mrs. Jung who was again staring at him. Looking at his        phone he sees Skrilla's Boo across the screen and opens the message that reads.

"Even though we might not want to, sometimes we have to let em go babe. Luv u!"

After reading the text his head drops down as if he was trying to put it on his lap. Mrs. Jung could sense something was troubling him and avoided asking him what he was doing hanging in the store, understanding that her store also dubbed as a hustler's refuge

during working hours. Her staring was quickly interrupted by the door swinging open and a new customer entering. Dressed in all black, it is the jewelry
store's first customer of the day stopping in for a cigar
to burn with an aura of nothing but trouble. He walks
in and looks over to Skrilla.

"Ill Skrillz! You aight partna? Do'n ya thing tonight
right playboy?!"

Skrilla looks up and realizes that he doesn't know
customer past seeing him around the way.

"Yeah I'm good fam."

"No diggy. No diggy." He says looking up at the
display of Chinese food on the sign.

"Yes, what do you want?!"

The customer continues to look at the sign and
says, "Uh...Just gimmie three bags of hot chips and a
homemade iced tea."

Mrs. Jung doesn't flinch until she sees him motion
towards his pocket and then pull out a roll of cash and
slides a bill through the slot.

"What I look like the type a nigga to haul ass out
the store wit some potato chips?! Fuck, I look like Pre-
cious to you?"

Mrs. Jung hands him his things and he walks to
the door.

"Aight Skrillz...be easy!"

"Aight dog."

The customer exits the store almost bumping into
Lil E who walks in before the door closes.

"What the fuck? Tell me something I want to here!"
Skrilla says to him, too drained to start screaming the
way he'd envisioned himself doing on his way to the
store.

"Dog I talked to my man right before I dropped you off. I was on the way to go check him but when I got over there, he ain't pick up, but I know he ain't gonna stiff us homie! For real! He's a good nigga!"

"Good nigga my ass! What kinda good nigga leaves other good niggaz on stuck like this?!"

"I feel you, but I got you. Wait till you see my man come through. I can show you better than I can tell you. He fuck around and be call'n me any minute fam. Just a little more faith in ya boy! You eat yet?"

"Man when I had time to eat?! Plus I'm broke I had to go get fresh for tonight."

"Man, order some shit my nig! Whatchu want? I got you."

The words "I got you" rang in Skrilla's head as he stood up off of the window sill feeling it was only right that he take him up on his offer, though part of him was trying to wrap his head around the fact that E still had money in his pocket while he on the other hand was stretched to the limit. Mrs. Jung stares at the two as their heads simultaneously look from right to left at the picture menu. After a few seconds of staring at the arrangement of Chinese dishes the two look at each other then and simultaneously say, "Chicken cheese".

"Yeah, yeah! What you two want?!"

"Let me get two chicken cheese steaks, fried onions."

"You pay now!"

"No, you make food now! I gotchu!" E says in his normal charismatic fashion, catching the attention of Skrilla. She snares at him with her eyeballs and calls the order to the kitchen in Chinese. Feeling like he was back in control, E lights another blunt in the store and Mrs. Jung begins to violently smack the window.

"No smoking in store!"

"Yeah aight! It smells better than that shit you cook'n!"

Skrilla gets up and heads to the door to exit followed by E. Immediately after stepping onto the curb Lil E. let's out a big cloud of smoke funking up the corner and replies.

"Yeah, she in there trip'n! I don't know why, all that bread they get'n in there."

"Man, I ain't talk'n bout her. I'm talk'n bout me nigga! All fuck'n day out here and no chain! Damn! Besides how you know she can't be stressed about money too? Who told you how much they make everyday? How you know they ain't got shit they gotta do too? I'm sittin' here watching you tell her when you gonna pay her too. Muthatfuckas kill me wit that shit! I never see ya'll go to McDonalds and tell them to make the food first, only in the hood ya'll do this shit!"

"Now I know you trip'n! Chill my nigga he come'n."

Skrilla looks down at the time on his phone that now reads 6:22. Losing all faith in his friend, he stumbles into a revelation and feels he's now been forced into plan b.

"Yeah aight man! Its cool, I know what I gotta do!"

A confused look takes over Lil E's face while the opposite look starts to mount on Skrilla's. He has become certain of what he has to do, this time leaving E in the dark where he often finds himself when E is at the wheel.

# Chapter Fourteen

Without an abundance of customers funneling into the store and the ones that did come in only browsing while seeking a brief refuge from the heat, Jessica is passing time flipping through a magazine on the counter. Eli is next to her stuffing a finished cigarette into an over crowded ash tray. Attempting to lighten the mood, Mark walks to the radio and taps the power button.

"It's much too quiet in here. Let me put this on."

"Please don't! I can't take it." Jessica says calmly without taking her eyes off of the magazine's pages. Nonchalantly turning another page, Mark refuses to allow the monotony to continue and persists.

"What's your station you like? We have to play something Mami."

"99..."

The workers continue doing much of nothing as the radio plays throughout the store. The song nears its end and the music is abruptly interrupted by the Dj who blasts onto the airwaves with some important news.

"Aight people, we only got about two and a half hours left until the sold out Career Criminals show begins!"

Mark, Eli, and Jessica all pause and listen to the radio. All motion stops in the store with Eli even stopping in his tracks on the way to the bathroom. The Dj continues, to address the city while the three hang on to his every word.

"What up ya'll?! This is Dj Astro Al with some important news for ya'll so listen up! You know we couldn't get the big dogs on the phone, but we did holler at the city's next big man in line earlier! That's right we talked to North Philly's own Skrilla Kay!! You know we couldn't hold him up too long, but he did tell us, fresh cut check, fresh gear check! And most of all that big ass chain is most definitely on check!!!

Mark quickly turns the radio down before exchanging a look of extreme disappointment with Eli, who now looks completely drained. At this point Mark can no longer hide his anguish and shake his true feelings from his face. The two look at each other and then look to Jessica.

"Jessica sweetheart, do me this favor and run the corner for me please and put change in the meter for Eli's car. Thank you Mami."

"It's after six. They won't ticket you. You're cool."

"No, no...Its just...Well you never know in this city, right?" He says dropping two quarters into her hand.

"Mmm hmmm!" She replies loud enough to infer that the two of them are full of shit and that she is fully aware that a private conversation has become necessary for them. She gets up and walks toward the door while Eli taps the buzzer for her to exit, taking a hard look at Mark wondering what he has something up his sleeve and is readying to let out.

Immediately after the door shuts Eli jumps the gun and bursts out.

"You see! Now do you see! He is not coming! But you know who is coming? Don't you?! Let me guess, all out of ideas now huh?! I can feel it, we're close to the end.

"Listen my brother. I did not plan for us to lose the store and I won't let us lose our store. We are better than this. You are right about many things Eli but this is one thing you are wrong about my brother."

Mark bends down and reaches behind one of the store's showcase and begins rummaging through some junk stored beneath it.

"Got it!" He yells, pulling a fairly old looking gun from the inside of a battered shoe box from the storage space below. Eli's face quickly wrinkles in confusion and astonishment.

"What are you still doing with that? You buy that from customer and don't know where it's been. I told you too get rid of that thing."

"You are right again! That's exactly why I kept it!" Responds Mark, confusing Eli even further.

"What, losing store is not enough for you? We must go to jail also?"

"No, listen, I kept this as an insurance policy. Look the chain is insured right? All we have to do is call police and tell them robber come inside and robbed us for the chain, and they dropped this! We will actually make money because our policy is for much more!"

103

Unwilling to consign his plan, but not wanting to talk him out of it either, Eli asks, "Now my friend I am certain America has made you lose your mind. Are you crazy!?!?"

"Yes, my brother, crazy about our dream!" Mark says, now donning a mildly sinister smile.

Jessica buzzes the door and re-enters feeling the weird air in the store, left only to wonder what had been said.

# Chapter Fifteen

Walking with Skrilla towards Big Chollie's block, a dangerous environment, even for those native to the neighborhood, Lil E. pleads with Skrilla to change his plans while beginning to understand the severity of the situation, feeling if he fumbled this mission his position in Skrilla's life would be redefined forever.

"Come on dog, you sure you wanna do this? We don't need nobody else in on this. We can't be letting outsiders in on our thing. How's that gonna look? Soon as this nigga hit me we shoot'n right there!"

"Man I don't need to here that shit no more! Save it! I'm gonna just ask Big Chollie to borrow the bread like I should've done this morning. Shit, yesterday! Last week, month!" Skrilla bursts back becoming more empowered with his every word. A sense of confidence takes over his stride, though beneath it all he is still walking over eggshells hoping his plan does not fall short.

"Skrillz you my guy from knee high. Come on man, I gotchu!"

"Yeah we're good, but you keep say'n you got me but you don't get me. You get me?!"

The two slow down just after crossing the street onto Chollie's block, a dark and dreary landscape with the street lights shot out to hide the block's nefarious activities. The street was lined with junkies and dealers alike and was known notoriously throughout the neighborhood as a strip you didn't want to walk on if you didn't have business there. In fact, it was also a strip you would prefer not to walk on if you did have business on. E and Skrilla's conversation has quieted as they approach an abandoned house with several unsavory workers outside sitting on the steps unimpressed with Skrilla's celebrity. Big Chollie's truck can also be seen outside of the house wit the engine running and music playing, though it is obvious that the truck is vacant.
In one final attempt to plead with Skrilla before they approach the workers outside the house E quietly mouths to him.

"Damn Skrillz, I don't know, word get out that Chollie bought that jawn and...."

"And what?! This nigga known me for ever! He used to hustle wit my brother when he was alive. Besides I ain't got no choice now do I?!"

E lets out a lung full of air follows closely behind his friend like a puppy following behind its owner as Skrilla steps to the men outside. Before any words could leave his mouth one of the men leaning on the wall of one of the streets abandoned rows ever so calmly looks to them and says.

"Who dat Skrilla? Damn, what's up Young G?" Breaking the ice and letting them know they were safe.

"What's up y'all? Is Chollie around? I wanted to holler at him for a sec."

"Who ya man?" He says after looking E up and down.

"Oh, this my nigga E, he cool."

The worker glances at Lil E again and then taps the leg of another worker sitting next to him.

"Go tell Chollie Skrilla out here dog."

"Good look'n Fam..." Skrilla says minding his manners on one of the grimiest blocks in his neighborhood.

The worker gets up and walks to the door of the house next to the abandoned one. Before he could get inside Big Chollie darts out in a rush with a slightly surprised look on his face as he spots Skrilla and E posted up on the wall with his crew. With an important mission to take care of the sight of the two isn't enough to break his stride to the truck while he greets them.

"Oh shit, Skrillz. Ya aight dog? What's good wit you? I'ma be over there fuck'n wit y'all tonight. My lil shorty got me a ghetto pass. I'ma holla later, matter fact young'n hook my nigga Skrillz up wit a half, on me. Aight fellas!"

The worker immediately follows the order and goes into the building to grab the work.

"Damn. Good look'n Chollie but I just wanted to holler a sec about..."

"Damn I wish I could but I'm already late for this drop. But I'm a definitely come fuck witchu in a lil bit dog, aight. Easy!" Chollie shouts from the window of his truck before turning the music up and peeling off down the street.

"Cool..." Skrilla says quietly realizing that there was know way possible for him to be heard by anyone other then the workers and his homie who was briefly relieved but feeling the pressure for him to show up was now at its peek. Skrilla watches the truck reach the corner as the man comes back out of the house.

"Don't worry fam. That shit happens to everybody. Chollie be on the move." He says handing Skrilla a balled up black plastic bag with a half ounce of weed that could be smelled through twenty of the bags that is was currently in.

Skrilla stares at the bag feeling completely deflated but responds cordially. "Aight fam, that's what's up."

"Aight my nigga...do ya thing tonight. If you anything we out here!"

"Aight fellas." E says to the crew receiving no response as he and Skrilla head off in the direction they had come from.

After reaching the corner and turning off of the block back into the light E comes alive again. He felt like a hustler again. Chollie's block had the ability to make even a certified hustler far above the status of Lil E feel like they were just playing in the game. It wasn't a block for jokes and hustler costumes. The workers out there weren't concerned with fresh clothes and haircuts, nor were they impressed by it. Their concerned lied with the constant flow of money, controlling the dope traffic that was their prominent source of income and protecting the block at all costs.

"Damn! You smell that shit we gonna light the sta-dium up tonight for real my nig! Whoo!"

"Here you go again! Bitches weed! What the fuck?! I can't even taste the shit cause a my p.o., and you know why I gotta p.o. right?!"

"My nigga, you know I ain't know it was stolen. Damn Skrillz."

Losing all control while they head back towards the Chinese restaurant, Skrilla turns to E and blurts out.

"Just do me one favor my nigga, one lil favor...a itty bitty fuck'n favor and answer me this. Can you do that? Where-the fuck-is ya man?! Tell me dat nigga!"

E sighs and slowly pulls out his phone and dials his man scared to death of what's to come.
Standing next to him, Skrilla is close enough to hear the call go straight to voicemail. E continues walking utterly speechless. They near the Chinese store and see the same shady customer in all black has re-turned and is standing outside of the restaurant again. At this point, Skrilla could absolutely care less who hears his conversation and is speaking as freely as he chooses.

"I don't fuck'n believe this shit nigga! You sup-posed to be my fuck'n dog! Instead of jus keep'n shit a hunnit and tell'n me I'm fucked! You wanna tease a nigga all fuck'n day. Like I'ma get paid! Damn, and I thought you was my man!"

"What!? Now I ain't ya nigga?!

"Shit, you tell me! This how you hold me down? What the fuck? What was I supposed to do, not bail my nigga out?! Let a nigga rot? You tell me it's coming back and then spend all the money except for the exact amount you owe me. And you do it right in front of my fuckin' face too! But if I ain't there for you then I ain't shit right?! I know!"

Lil E. is all out of rebuttals and drowning in his own shame, a first for someone with his level of confidence.

They pause outside of the restaurant confused about their next move, when their confusion is spotted and interrupted by this shady individual once again.

"What's good fellas? Holla at a nigga. Y'all niggaz look'n like y'all got a problem and y'all know I keeps the problem solver." He says tapping his waste where his gun sat snugly under his shirt.

Lil E looks at Skrilla and without comment steps toward the guy. Skrilla stops him, looking to prevent any added trouble to their situation that evening.

"Whatchu do'n?!"

Lil E looks Skrilla in the eye with a serious look equal to the one that led them onto Chollie's block. He realized just as E had realized earlier that there was nothing that could stop what was about to happen from happening.

"Look nigga I'm your street cred. I gotchu!" He says before walking into the store with the customer.

Skrilla stands out front watching through window the two inside talking and nodding their heads in agreement. He wanted no parts of what was going on but could only wonder what his friend was up to and if it would save the day, which he desperately wanted. He watches the body language of the character in all black grow more serious in nature as Lil E comes to the door inviting him in.

"Yo Skrillz!"

"Fuck it." Skrilla mumbles under his breath, turning around and walking into the restaurant.

# Chapter Sixteen

Back in the Jewelry box, Jessica waits around for the day to finally end and is becoming increasingly annoyed as the day drags on. She is well aware of a budding disagreement brewing between Eli and Mark who have been going back and fourth with each other about the robbery in mostly Russian. The argument begins to heat up as Mark defends his position firmly, letting Eli know his mind has been made up.

"Look this is our only option. I could see if we had no other options but we still have this one left. Of course we use it!"

"You are crazy! I'm not letting you take me to jail!"

"Have faith my brother!"

Jessica interrupts the Russian conversation, speaking in the international language of money, reminding them that she's in the room no matter how invisible their struggles have lead them to believe she is.

"I hope y'all talk'n bout my money! Cause I need to get paid!"

Mark returns to his normal voice attempting to smooth things over and stall her a little longer until his plan comes to fruition. Although he is as unsure as the weather he speaks with confidence trying to set everyone at ease, Eli especially.

"Of course you will, just maybe not tonight, but definitely tomorrow!"

Jessica's mouth opens wide in disbelief as Mark moves over to the register. Eli maintains a strong degree of eye contact with him trying to signal him to abort his insane mission that he believes will soon blow up in all of their faces, ultimately transforming into the end of their business venture in America and possibly the bringing about the beginning of a new career in the Philadelphia prison system. Speaking in Russian, Eli makes one more vail attempt to stop him.

"I cannot let you do this!"

Unwilling to let go of the dream and feeding into the do anything to succeed nature of North Philly, Mark looks him directly in the eye and taps the stores silent alarm button and says, "Lets just see what happens...right?". Eli smacks a nearly empty coffee cup off of the counter waiting to see what happens next now that what's done has been done. No turning back as the Jewelry Box enters a next phase in its evolution. Jessica hadn't witnessed him hitting the button but can tell that the situation was far more serious than she was lead to believe. All three are left in the dark as to what's to come but only Mark and Eli can spot the elephant dancing in the room as the evening continues.

# Chapter Seventeen

Meanwhile, as the sun sets, so does the mind of Manny who is now squatting down in the alley with a white tube sock covering his right hand. His sense of frustration was completely gone and replaced with an air of focus. He was taking his destiny into his own hands, even if it meant him molding it into a disaster. All that mattered is that it was one of his would be one of his own creation. The four corners that had become his entire world were now being controlled by the crews up the street that had infringed on what he had built and he finally had what he believed was a clear path to victory. A short sum of money was all that stood between him and reclaiming his end of the street and more importantly re-securing his legacy. With that in mind, he squatted down loading shells into the clip of his .45, preparing to take back what was his.

Skrilla and Lil E. slowly pull up two blocks away from the Jewelry Box where their new associate slams the clip of his gun into the handle of a large desert eagle and hops out of the car, closing the door and heading towards the store. Without receiving a head nod, a wink, or anything to confirm that they were in sync, E and Skrilla sat quietly in the car hoping things turned out well for them, E especially, knowing this was his last shot and their friendship was hanging in the balance.

Meanwhile Mark stands in the mirror of the store's bathroom looking himself in the eye while holding his trusty handgun up and cocking it. He is fully in the moment and beginning to feel like this was business as usual for the North Philadelphian he'd become. The small degree of fear ascended from his body and was replaced with the confidence of one of Big Chollie's workers, ready to defend his block at all costs. After placing the gun in his waste band he drops the bottom of his now wrinkled dress shirt down over it and exits the bathroom with the eye of the tiger intent on securing his American dream.

Outside of the store in his minivan, Mr. Jung sits quietly staring at a small .22 caliber pistol that fits snugly in the palm of his hand with a look of desperation covering his face. As he looked into the definition of the guns features he thought of his nagging wife and mother in law, and also of the life that he wanted for his children. He had know idea what he was about to do while sliding the gun into his pocket and stepping out of the van heading to the store to buzz the door.

Mr. Jung stands outside of the store looking thru the glass directly at Jessica and is buzzed in by Eli whom acted too quickly and hit the buzzer out of shock. Mr. Jung walks to the counter quickly trying to asses the body language of everyone in the store in a matter of seconds. Jessica's eyes begin to widen wondering what lie they will tell and if i will be enough to change the mind of Mr. Jung, who looks to be not in the mood for anything other than the payment that is owed to him. Eli takes a step back, caught off guard by Mr. Jung's timing and allowed Mark to step up to work his magic. All he was missing was his popcorn as he prepared for the show his friend was about to put on. Judging by the looks on the employees faces Mr. Jung could sense that his money had not yet arrived and opened up with a great deal of restraint in his voice.

"Ok fellas, just here for the rent."

"Uh...Good evening Mr. Jung. Actually, there's been a slight situation, and we're waiting for police as we speak."

Having absolutely no idea of what was going on, Jessica rolls her eyes and gets up heading to the back of the store. She believed that the mention of the police was a wild lie that Mark had concocted that very second and didn't want to sit in the middle of the argument that she felt was sure to come.

"No! I'll take the rent now. I have some other things to do tonight guys." He said, refusing to accept Mark's words as the outcome of this trying day.

"Yes, Mr. Jung, you are not understanding the circumstances in our store this evening. There has been a situation, a very serious situation!"

Eli stands with his arms crossed firmly, completely ashamed of what Mark is doing and rapidly becoming fearful of the madness being orchestrated.

"You are saying you don't have the rent! That's what you are saying!!"

Walking past Mr. Jung while talking, Mark opens the door and steps out of the store onto the curb looking left and right for the police to show up. Seizing the moment Eli signals Jessica to get her things and prepare to leave the store before the commotion that was to come.

"Let's get our things Ms. Jessica!" Eli says, snapping at Jessica as

Mr. Jung follows Mark onto the sidewalk outside of the store where he is again addressed by Mark.

"Mr. Jung! You really must understand the situation has become more difficult, but you will receive every penny owed to you, but right now this is matter for police!"

"Nonsense! I've waited long enough! Rent is due now, no more excuses!

"Mr. Jung, not now! Please Mr.Jung!" Mark asserts.

Mr. Jung becomes infuriated at the tone Mark has taken with him feeling bullied and slides his hand into his pocket wrapping it around the handle of his gun.

Directly above the store, the window of Mr. Jung's apartment is quietly raised just as the hooded robber creeps up to the gentlemen with his gun drawn.

"Back inside fellas!" He says with the nozzle of the gun inches away from a frozen Mr. Jung's head.

Mark immediately and instinctively whips the gun off of his waste and points it at the head of the robber.

"Hey, what are you doing homie?!" He says with his gun aimed directly at robber's nose creating and unforeseen opposition for the robber, Mr. Jung, as well as himself as the situation turns up a notch outside of the Jewelry Box making the streets hotter than the weather ever could.

# Chapter Eighteen

Spotting the standoff from their vantage point, Skrilla and E pause in shock at what they're witnessing.

"Oh shit! Come on, lets get outta here!" Skrilla says smacking the leg of Lil E with the back of his hand frantically, with making it the show being his only concern.

"Hold up a sec. Let's see where this is going." E responds, looking to crawl out of the hole he'd dug for he and his partner.

Unaware of what was transpiring Jessica opens the door to the store and immediately grips a small canister of mace and joins the standoff.

"Don't move Punto!" Jessica spouts off with her tone unleashing the native North Philly demeanor that was often suppressed by her softer side.

With the interruption that Jessica had quickly inserted the robber turns his arm and aims at Mark. With the gun now pointed somewhere other than his direction, Mr. Jung quickly pulls his weapon on the robber in another shocking turn of events.

Speeding around the corner like a man on a mission, a fully dressed Manny pulls up and drops his bike on the ground with a bandana covering his face, joining the party by taking out his gun and aiming it directly at an unarmed Eli whose arms fly into the air and remain frozen.

"You already know what it is!"

From the Jung's open window above, out slides a tech-nine firmly in the hands of Grandma Jung aimed at Mr Jung joining the madness as well. With his finger on the trigger itching to squeeze, the robber tries to regain control and take back his position as the grimiest character amongst them.

"Aight Fuck Dat, all y'all back in the store! What y'all think I'm play'n?!"

"Rent is due now!" Mr. Jung yells.

"I don't know what the fucks go'n on but my sister better get her two hunnit!" Adds Manny.

"What the fuck?!" Jessica says knowing exactly who was behind the bandana.

The commotion grows louder and louder as native tongues begin to fly. The thought of compromise has completely dissipated and a dangerous situation is growing more dangerous by the second. An astonished Skrilla and Lil E sit back and watch from the car.

"You seeing what I'm seeing!? Come on we out!" Skrilla says to E accepting their now apparent reality while signaling to pull off.

"Hold up Homie."

"Oh shit, look, look! Now it's definitely over!" Skrilla says spotting a police car flying onto the block signaling the end of the madness. The officers come to a screeching halt stopping just short of the armed argument. Jumping out of their vehicle and positioning themselves behind the open doors of their car, the two officers draw their weapons and shout to the crowd.

"Everybody freeze!"

Everyone simultaneously stops and looks at the officers for a strong two-seconds and then resume their native tongue arguments completely ignoring the presence of the police. This time much louder than before Chinese, Russian, Spanish, English, and North Phillyian resonates from the block sounding more like a disagreement in the United Nation's building.

From the inside of E's Caprice, Skrilla and E look on in utter amazement as the commotion ensues, when out of nowhere E flies the driver's side door open and jumps out of the car heading straight towards the ruckus.

"What the fuck?! Man!" He says with his pace quickly evolving into a run.

"What's up?!" Skrilla says to him flying his door open also.

Lil E is now racing towards the commotion with Skrilla following a few short paces behind him frantically yelling at him!

"Yo! Yo! Come on! I don't fuck'n need this! Fuck!

Just before reaching the confrontation Lil E veers off, revealing that he wasn't running to them and was actually running towards the dvd man who had just entered the block with his duffel bag over his shoulder and a look of astonishment garnering his face. Skrilla stops completely baffled as Lil E approaches the man.

"Yo what the fuck nigga, you try'n to play me?! What's up witchu??!!"

"Huh? I been look'n for you." He replies to E with his eyes remaining on the overblown confrontation a few feet away from them.

"Man stop play'n nigga, what's up?!"

"Chill! I don't know what's going on out here but chill."

At this point Skrilla can't resist jumping into the conversation to find out who E is running up on and why he's speaking so aggressively to him.

"Yo who this?!" Skrilla asks E with his eyes grilling the dvd man intensely.

"This my man!"

"Hold up, what??!! That's ya man?! Nigga!"

The DVD man calmly reaches into his pocket and pulls a roll of money out handing it to Lil E while shaking his head.

"Chill nigga, I been try'n to get wit you! Matter fact I told you to get wit me this morning! My phone died at like 5:00, but I told you all day!"

Skrilla looks at Lil E fwith steam emanating from him and takes the money.

"I ain't know Skrilla was ya man like that! You shoulda said that! This nigga gotta show to git to!"

E remains quiet after being exposed to his friend for not doing all that he could have to expedite the days process. Skrilla shakes his head at Lil E with a smirk after taking the money from him E finally opens up looking him in the eye and telling him, "I told you I got you homie!" Skrilla immediately turns toward the standoff yelling over them all while waving the cash in the air for them all to see.

"Chill, chill! Everybody hold up! I got the bread! Chill!"

One of the officers locks Skrilla into his sights with his gun drawn trying to figure out what he is attempting to do. The arguing dies down as the participants all take notice to the much needed cash being waved in front of them as they begin to lower their weapons and pay closer attention to Skrilla.

With much more important things to do, Skrilla bravely walks directly in between the armed North Philadelphians and slaps the money into Mark's hand with a smile that he is unable to control.

"Hey, my man Skrilla! Yes, I knew you'd come!"

Mr. Jung takes a hard look at the money in Mark's hand and begins to loudly clear his throat catching Mark's attention. Looking to Mr. Jung Mark says "You see Mr. Jung, you are not forgotten. Here is your money as promised!" Mr Jung is now next in line with the chain reaction of smirks going around sliding the money as well as his gun into his pocket.

"Hold up Chino! My sister needs her two hunnit!" Manny says abruptly from behind his bandana, again revealing his true identity to everyone.

"Oh I almost forgot! I'm sorry, Mr. Jung could you please...." Mark mutters.

Mr. Jung peels off two hundred dollars and hands it to Jessica who begins smiling at Mark. In the midst of the new events Eli had stepped back into the store and gone behind the counter for Skrilla's chain and had now returned with it in hand sparkling and lighting up the corner. All guns have been lowered including the tech nine grandma Jung had quietly slid back into the window above the store. The only guns that remained drawn were the ones the police were handling and the one of the robber who was now the only one locked into their targets. Realizing what was going on the robber grows extremely angry and decides to turn up the heat.

"Nah, nah fuck that! Everybody happy but me?! Give me that fuck'n chain!" He says turning the gun on Skrilla who finally has his chain in its rightful place around his neck. Lil E looks at Skrilla and takes a deep breath before springing into action.

"Nah fuck that, I'm yo street cred!" He says just before jumping out and slapping the arm of the robber down trying to knock the gun from his hand. The weapon discharges and the bullet grazes Skrilla's arm as the rookie cop shouts out, "I'm hit" with the bullet entering his shoulder.

Jessica instinctively sprays the robber in the face with a pool's worth of mace and kicks him in the genitals.

"Take that Punto!"

The other officer takes his shot, hitting him in the elbow forcing him to drop his gun on the pavement. It seems the madness is now over and things begin to go back into their normal order with everyone satisfied including the cops who are ignoring the fact that there is weapon on the waste of almost everyone out there. Sirens begin to blare as the clean up crew arrives and starts to pick up the pieces.

The Robber sits handcuffed in the back of an ambulance with the medics roughly attending to his arm. Just a car's length away the officer lies on a stretcher in the back of another parked ambulance with his partner standing over him smiling.

"Man, stripes on your first day! I've been try'n to get shot since I started! Rook, your a natural!"

The cop rolls his eyes at his partner as Mr. Jung, Mark and Eli look on from the curbside. The three all shake hands reconciling with each other.

"Next month you on time...Eh fellas?"

"Of course Mr. Jung, of course."

Eli smiles at Mark and puts hand on his shoulder slightly squeezing it.

"You did my brother."

"No, we did it! Another day closer to our dream my brother."

Unable to resist the moment, Manny looks to his sister and opens up.

"Um..Uh..You know I love you Sis?!"

"Yeah I know, you crazy ass!...Here" She says placing the much needed two hundred dollars into his hands lighting up his face.

"Thanks Sis! I'm bout to get the block back y'all!" He shouts before quickly covering his mouth with his hand noticing he's in ear shot of the police and probably shouldn't be announcing his plans.

Skrilla and Lil E are now leaning on the back of a parked car unwinding and taking in the scenery of the dying commotion on Germantown Avenue.

"Damn my nigga, it's been a long day! Shit is crazy!"

"That's for sure my nigga! That's real rap!"

"Could've been a lot shorter tho!" Skrilla adds while laughing.

"Yeah I know Skrillz. I told you I gotchu King!" E replies returning the laughter.

"Lets go tear this thing down my G!" Skrilla says giving E a pound, letting him know there was no love lost.

"For sho homie!" E replies with his eyes locked onto Jessica.

"Yo Skrillz, you head to car I'll be right there."

Skrilla shakes his head chuckling and heading off towards the car knowing that not much has changed with E at all. He took a few steps away and turned around only to notice E had Jessica smiling already. Skrilla reached the car and hopped in waiting for his homie to hurry up once again as the dvd man passed by the car saying to him. "Yo Skrillz, where's ya man?" Skrilla smiled and pointed up the block to E who was exchanging numbers with Jessica. The dvd man looked and replied "Ahh, I'll get with him tomorrow. Do ya thing tonight G!"

"For sho!"

Skrilla was now about to enter the realm of frustration again waiting on E when he came jogging down the block and hopped in the car.

"I think I'm in love!"

Skrilla looked at him and rolled his eyes while turning on the radio as they pull off of the block. Coincidentally the Dj comes on the speaker loudly blasting into his mic.

"Whats up Philly that Career Criminals show is indeed go'n down! Ya heard! Also we heard thru the grapevine it got kinda crazy out there in the streets of North Philly tonight! Apparently my man Skrilla Kay was in an altercation while picking his chain up from being cleaned and some fool tried to rob the place! My man Skrilla was grazed in the arm but he still show'n up to grace the stage! North Philly style y'all!"

"That's crazy!" The two say simultaneously as they head onto Broad Street sharing a much needed laugh together getting ready to shut shit down, North Philly style of course!

# "Special Thanks to Alym & Amazia"

### with Love
### Daddo & Uncle Jus

# Don't forget to get your copy of The Manual by Jus One today!!!

# Available Now!!!